BLAZE

THE PHOENIX PROPHECY
BOOK TWO

CARA CLARE

Blaze
Copyright © 2022 Cara Clare.

The moral rights of the author have been asserted.
All rights reserved.

No part of this book may be reproduced, stored in a retrieval system, or transmitted in any form or by any means, electronic, mechanical, photocopying, recording, or otherwise, without the prior written permission of the publisher or copyright holder, except in the case of brief quotations embodied in critical articles or reviews.

This edition firstpublished in Great Britain in 2025 by **Arcane Passion Press, an imprint of A.P Beswick Publications.**

Publishing rights are held by **A.P Beswick Publications** under license from the author.

ISBN (Paperback): 978-1-916671-65-2
ISBN (Hardback): 978-1-916671-66-9

A.P Beswick Publications
Oswaldtwistle Mills Business Centre, Clifton Mill, Pickup Street, Accrington, BB5 0EY
Cover Design: Beautiful Book Covers by Ivy

*For all the Novas who are ready
for their sparks to fly.*

THE PHOENIX PROPHECY SERIES

Book One: Nova
Book Two: Blaze
Book Three: Ashes
Book Four: Embers
Book Five: Flames
Book Six: Fire Bird
Book Seven: Blood
Book Eight: Ice
Book Nine: Snow

Prequel novella: Hollow

Books 1-6 can be read as a complete story arc.
Books 7-9 follow Nova and the guys as they face a new threat.

When above turns to darkness
And below breaks free
A witch born to humans
Salvation shall bring
Fated to five who are not what they seem
The Phoenix will rise and become Earth's Queen
Into the embers
One
Two
Three
Devoured by Flame
The Phoenix is She

1

NOVA

A crackle of heat staccatos down my arm into my fingers. Sparks dance on the phone's edges, but I grip it tightly. I'm staring at the screen, reading the message over and over.

We have the seer. Come alone or he won't live to see tomorrow.

Every muscle in my body is pulsing. Heat is filling me up, burning my skin from the inside out. Rage and fear swirl in my stomach.

They have Kole. Someone has taken him. But who are they?

My legs shudder with the urge to run downstairs and straight into Tanner's arms. I picture thrusting the phone at Mack, imagine him showing the message to Luther as I tell Tanner what it said, then see the vengeful thirst in their faces as they tell me they'll get Kole back and that no one will hurt him.

But the message said *alone*.

Come alone or he dies.

"Nova? You coming?" Tanner's voice drifts up from the hall. With it wafts the smell of Mack's cooking. A few minutes ago, I was ravenous. Now, nausea has settled in my throat and the thought of eating makes my head spin.

"Just a minute," I call back, lowering myself onto the top step before I pass out.

Beside me, a large floor-to-ceiling window frames a view of The Hollow's perfect lawn. The fountain, the trees. Above the treeline, the sky is brightening. It's caught halfway between blue and pink. A color I can't name.

Franklin Warehouse, sunset.

Sunset is twelve hours away.

I read the message again and look at the number it came from. I don't recognize it, but my thoughts are slowing now. I can't afford to panic, even though whatever magickal force has bonded me to Kole is making me feel like there's a swarm of ants under my skin trying to burrow their way to the surface.

What would Mack or Luther do first? They're cops. They wouldn't jump in, no matter how much they wanted to. I exhale forcefully and try to center myself.

Mack would make sure the message was real before deciding on a course of action.

As my panic clears a little, another thought settles; Kole is powerful. He's a huge Viking of a mage. It would take an army to capture him.

A tentative glimmer of hope lights in my chest. Perhaps it is a hoax after all.

Slowly, I type out a reply. *Who is this? I need proof you have him.*

Then I dial Kole's number. It rings and rings, but he doesn't pick up. Our relationship has never exactly been the calling, texting type. But I know he'd answer if he saw my name flashing on the screen. I try the bar. No answer there either. I stare at the phone, then I text him. *Call me. Urgent.*

"Nova? You okay?" Tanner's head appears at the bottom of the stairs. He's peering up at me, a concerned expression on his face that makes my stomach roll with the need to open up to him and tell him what's happening.

When he sees I'm sitting down, and presumably the expression on my face, he sprints up the stairs two at a time to crouch in front of me. The shade of his shirt makes his eyes sparkle. No one has ever looked at me the way he looks at me; like he'd die if I was hurt and kill whoever caused my pain.

"Did something happen?" He rests his palm gently on my upper thigh. Usually, when he touches me, I lean into him. As if he can never be close enough. But right now, all I can think is that he's an empath; figuring out feelings is what he does. So, if I lie to him, he will know.

Keeping the message from him is a betrayal. He cares for me and Kole. He should know, but I'm almost paralyzed by the idea that telling him could put Kole in more danger.

I'm holding my phone in my lap. When Tanner glances at it, I force a smile to my lips and shove it into my pocket. One step at a time; I need to know the message was real before I decide what to do. So, hoping that staying close to the truth might mask what I'm not telling him, I say, "Sorry. I just got a weird message. It freaked me out a bit."

A steeliness comes to Tanner's eyes. Their sparkle darkens. "What message? Let me see."

"It's fine. Nothing to worry about. Probably a prank. Some weirdo. Wrong number." I stand, trying to keep my voice light and nonchalant even though I know I'm talking too quickly. *No big deal. Nothing to see here.* I repeat the thought, hoping its essence will envelop me and hide my true feelings.

"What did it say? This message?" Tanner looks at my pocket as if he's expecting me to take out my phone and show him. "We need to be careful, Nova. That video…" Tanner follows me as I trot down the stairs. When I don't answer him, he catches my elbow and says, "Nova, what kind of prank?"

His touch is light but I flinch.

He immediately softens and bites his lower lip as he studies me. Is he searching my emotions right now?

"Seriously, Tan, it's fine." I steel myself, then turn to him and smile. Slotting my arms under his, I loop them around his torso and nuzzle under his chin. "But I like it when you get all protective. It's super cute."

I'm behaving the way I used to with Johnny, using a sultry voice and sweet words to divert attention from what I'm thinking. I hate that I'm doing this with Tanner. My relationship with him is nothing like my relationship with Johnny, or like any other I've had. It's different, perfect, and beautiful. I don't want it to be tainted.

For a moment, Tanner's muscles remain taut. Tears have sprung to my eyes, but I blink them away quickly before he can see. If he feels them, he doesn't let me know it. He simply kisses my forehead, his lips like a snowflake settling on my fiery skin. "You're my girl. I'd do anything to protect you." He steps back a little and meets my eyes, nudging my chin with his thumb. "You know that, right?"

"Of course." I'm trying not to think about the message. Pushing thoughts of Kole and what's happening to him into the basement of my mind until it's safe to feel them without Tanner knowing. If that's even the way it works; in truth, I have no idea how his powers affect him. I don't know if he feels without meaning to or if he can shut it on and off.

"You're sure it's nothing to worry about?" He smiles with the corner of his mouth. It dimples his cheek.

"Trust me." I blink up at him, hating myself for saying 'trust me' while hiding something so huge.

Tanner nods slowly. "Okay, but—" Before he can ask anything else, I duck around him and head for the kitchen, trotting down the stairs as if I'm starving and excited about breakfast. I'm not sure whether I've fooled him or if it's blindingly obvious that I'm masking something. If it is, he's not letting on.

"Morning, you two." Mack greets us as we enter the kitchen. Early morning sun shines through the windows. He's opened the doors and a cool breeze is mingling with the smells coming from the stove. He puts a pot of coffee down on the table and gestures for us to sit. "Nova..." He stands back, hands in his pockets in a way that would have drawn my attention to his crotch if I wasn't so distracted. "How are you? After last night?"

My mind stumbles on the question. Images pummel through me. The cellar. Kole. My legs on his shoulders as he—

"Not sure she's up for talking about it, Prof." Tanner puts his arm around me and raises his eyebrows at Mack. "It was a lot." They're not talking about Kole or what happened in the cellar; they're talking about my family and what I did to them.

Instead of trying to push them away, I let the memories of my parents' screams surface. I let myself see my foster brother's face; a face I blocked out for so very long.

I won't block them out anymore; they deserve to be remembered.

"Of course." Mack smiles. It makes his eyes crinkle. He takes a hand from his pocket and rubs his neat gray beard.

I close my eyes, let the memories ebb, then look from Mack to Tanner. My heart is throbbing in my chest. I want so badly to tell them about the message, to ask what I should do, but fear has welded my jaw shut.

"Hungry?" Mack asks.

I nod, even though I'm not.

As Tanner heads to the stove to help Mack serve the food, I pour myself a mug of coffee and wrap my hands around it. I add three spoonfuls of sugar. I'm staring at the slowly swirling liquid when I feel Luther enter the room.

He brings with him a heat that makes the air shift. He's a fire mage, which means he has powers like mine. The difference is, he knows how to use his. When I turn to greet him, he simply tips his chin at me and stalks over to speak to Mack. Despite what we learned from Kole's vision, his dislike for me doesn't seem to have mellowed.

The three of them are deep in hushed conversation when my phone vibrates. With shaking fingers, I take it from my pocket and shield it from view as I unlock the screen.

A video. They sent me a video.

I stand quietly and slip from the room. Outside, at the top of the stone steps, I press play.

2

KOLE

It's pitch dark, but my eyes are open. I know this blackness; a blinding spell. A powerful one.

I try to move my limbs. I can feel them—arms behind my back, feet flat on the floor—but it's as if they're made of lead. I blink slowly and will my heartbeat to slow until the pounding in my veins blends with the rumbling of an engine. I'm in some kind of vehicle. A van. Traveling at high speed, the vibrations coursing up through my feet into my legs. I'm not alone. Whoever else is here, they're trying hard not to be noticed, but I can hear their shallow breaths. Three different rhythms.

So, there are three of them.

Three of them and one of me.

Kayla's face fills my mind. The familiar snarl that curls her upper lip. The scar that weaves a jagged line from her right eyebrow to her jaw. Always an angry purple, despite the fact it's been years since it was fresh.

She's not one of the three; I'd feel her if she was.

Whoever they are, I'm not going to give them the satisfaction of seeing me struggle. The spells restraining me are powerful. I could break them if I had to, but I'm weak. There's something foreign in my veins, fogging my thoughts. Whatever Pete put in my drink, it was strong stuff. It's left a bitter, acidic taste in my mouth.

"Don't bother to fight." A voice I don't recognize breaks through the blackness. Female. Younger than Kayla, but older than Nova.

Nova's name zigzags through my bones.

Nova.

Something's coming.

The female is closer now. I can feel her breath on my cheek. "It'll take every ounce of strength you've got to break my spells. By the time you manage it, you'll be so spent that I'll be able to lock you back up with nothing more than a click of my fingers."

I don't speak. Her hand is on my thigh.

I don't allow my jaw to twitch. Don't give away anything that would betray the fact I feel like severing this witch's hand from her wrist with my teeth so she can never touch me again.

Nova is the only woman who should be touching me.

Nova.

Something's coming.

"We're nearly there, Ink Heart." The female is no longer in front of me but, as she speaks, her words seem louder.

Ink Heart. It's been years since anyone called me that; it's a name I prayed I'd never have to hear again.

"Kayla's told us so much about you." There's a clunk as the witch sits back down. Heavy boots on the metal floor of the van. "Despite your betrayal, you're somewhat legendary in League folklore We're very excited to find out if the stories are all true."

I say nothing.

"Eve, watch what you're saying. We're not here to reminisce." A gruff male voice, clearly a werewolf, interrupts the witch's taunting.

"Can we tell him why?" Eve asks, her voice bright and excited, like a child waiting to open their Christmas presents.

"No. Kayla won't be pleased if you play with her toy."

"But she's already played with him. I want a turn," Eve whines.

Another male wolf, younger than the first, huffs and says, "Eve, get a hold of yourself. Don't you witches have any self-control?"

"*You're* talking to *me* about self-control? The wolf who devoured a human last week when he was supposed to be capturing them? Because he couldn't control his *urges?*"

"Shut the fuck up, Eve." The young wolf's tone darkens.

As they start to bicker, I tune them out and try to latch onto anything, any sound, that might tell me where we are or where we're heading. I search for the sound of a train, the falls, kids playing in a schoolyard, or music filtering out of bars, but there's nothing strong enough to latch onto except the sound of the road. Smooth and straight. A highway. I don't know what direction we're traveling in, how long we've been on the road, or if it's still daylight outside.

The only thing I know for sure is that we're traveling away from Phoenix Falls. I can feel it—the chasm that's growing between me and Nova.

A sickening heat washes over me as I picture her face. The way she looked when she came to the cellar. The thirst in her eyes.

I knew in that moment what had happened; I just don't know how it happened. A blood bond forms when a human tastes a super's blood. She didn't taste me. But I know we are bound together. I know I am meant to be near her, with her, inside her, protecting her.

Hunger swirls in my throat. The need for her is all-consuming, more powerful than anything I've ever felt. More than The Hunger. More than lust or love.

My thoughts snag and falter. I know nothing about Kayla's witch and what she can do. Few have the power to read thoughts, but if she can and if she does… she cannot know about the blood bond. She cannot know about Nova.

I take a long, slow breath, inhaling so that the rise of my chest is barely visible. I need Nova out of my head.

A thunderous growl shakes the belly of the van. It's the older wolf putting the younger one in his place. "Enough!" He snarls. "Both of you. Not another word until we stop."

The younger wolf whimpers.

The witch doesn't seem fazed but shuts up all the same.

There's silence for several long minutes. Just the sound of the van. Then it begins to slow. It turns off the highway and the road changes. Tarmac turns to dirt, something rougher and louder.

The witch claps her hands together. "We're here!"

And suddenly, I can see.

3

MACK

Nova looks exhausted when she walked into the kitchen. I had to fight the urge to stride over, wrap her in my arms, and kiss her. Run my hands over her curves, breathe in every inch of her.

I wanted to do it last night. When I heard her in the shower with Tanner, I wanted to push the door open and help him soothe her. Fill her up until there was no room left for the anguish that tormented her.

But that's his job, not mine. I'll have to think of other ways to take care of her.

"Mack?" Tanner nudges me. He's holding a plate, ready for me to load eggs onto it.

I nod and serve up two large spoonsful. I'm adding bacon when Luther stalks in. He's simmering, pissed about something. He thumps the worktop with his fist when he reaches us.

"Still can't get that fucking video taken down. I've called every hacker I know, but it's everywhere. As soon as one disappears, another pops up." He grits his teeth. He must have been up all night. "And it gets worse."

I put down the pan and fold my arms, angling away from Nova even though she seems too lost in thought to hear what we're saying.

Lowering his voice, Luther meets my gaze. "I just got a call from the station. The bus driver recognized her. He called the Ridgemore cops, then every news outlet he could think of… they know she came to Phoenix Falls."

I don't feel fear very often but, at this moment, a lightning rod of the stuff shoots down my spine. Snow shudders with the urge to take over and start breaking things. I look over Luther's shoulder. Nova is outside staring at the fountain, her back to the kitchen.

"It's been on the news?"

Luther nods grimly and swipes his palm over his closely shaved head. When I first met him, he was a twenty-something-year-old with thick, black hair. He shaved it when he graduated. "Might be time to call the Bureau, Mack," he says darkly. "Before long, every news anchor and cop in the state will be on our doorstep."

I close my eyes. As soon as I saw that video, I knew we'd have to involve the Bureau eventually. I just hoped we could get a few more facts under our belts first. "You're right."

"What?" Tanner's eyes widen. "I thought you said the Bureau's changed. That we don't know who we can trust."

"If we don't call them, they'll call us." Inside my head, Snow rumbles in agreement. "They know about the prophecy. They know we're in Phoenix Falls for a reason. When they see a human on TV, setting fire to her deadbeat boyfriend, then hear that she got on a bus to our town, they'll connect the dots. If they haven't already."

Tanner's shoulders are shaking with tension. Luther puts a firm hand on his back. "She'll be okay, Tanner. We won't let anything happen to her."

"Since when do you care?" Tanner bites back, then screws his eyes shut and sighs. "Sorry, man. I didn't mean that."

"Look, I know I'm not her biggest fan," Luther says sincerely, "but after last night, I believe she's important. Plus, you're my brother and she's your girl. So, I'm going to help you take care of her. Right?"

Tanner nods. "Right." He hesitates. He's canted his head in her direction and his eyes have narrowed.

"What is it?" I ask; he might be the empath, but I've known him long enough now to know when he's holding something back.

Tanner looks from me to Luther. "She's hiding something," he says quietly.

Luther raises an eyebrow.

"Not like that. Not like when she came here. Something else. I can't catch hold of it. She's doing everything she can to stop me from feeling it, but I don't want to go looking too deep. It doesn't feel like something a boyfriend should do."

I'd have to agree with him there; using your powers to read loved ones' thoughts and feelings is never a good idea. "Have you asked her?" I rub my beard, watching Nova through the open door as the breeze catches her silver hair.

Tanner shakes his head then he takes a deep breath and says quietly, "She formed a blood bond with Kole. I don't know how. She didn't taste his blood, but it happened. They both feel it. She went down to the cellar last night and…" He trails off and sighs, pushing his fingers through his hair and raising his eyebrows.

"Kole fucked her?" Luther asks bluntly. I wince at his phrasing.

"No. I was with them. He didn't, but there was…" Under other circumstances, Tanner's eyes would be dancing as he told us the details, but now all I see is worry. "She seemed good this morning, though. When we woke up, she was happy, joking with me." He pauses, then adds, "She said she got a weird message. Some kind of prank. That's when she started holding something back."

I take my eyes away from Nova and place a firm hand on Tanner's shoulder. He's never dated properly before, and certainly never been in love, so there's a distinct possibility this is an emotional, relationship-based problem and not a prophecy-based one.

"Tanner," I say firmly, trying not to sound too much like a father or an uncle, "talk to her. Maybe she's confused about what happened. Maybe she's scared about the blood bond. They're powerful. She's had a lot to deal with in the last twenty-four hours."

To my surprise, Luther chips in, "Mack's right. Things between the two of you got heavy pretty fast. Maybe she feels guilty because she cares about you and now she's got all these twisted, suped-up feelings for Kole. Humans find the notion of sharing confusing at the best of times." He nods. "Don't freak until you've spoken to her."

Tanner forces a smile. "Right."

Luther gestures to the table. "Kole went to a meeting after I let him out. He said he'll be back. Maybe the three of you should talk while Mack and I go to the station and make some calls."

Again, Tanner says, "Right. We'll talk." But he's lost in thought. He looks gray around the edges.

When Nova walks back into the kitchen, she smiles at him, and he kisses her. What he doesn't see is that she's gripping her phone so tightly that her knuckles have whitened.

Whatever's going on here, it's not about her feelings for Tanner or Kole. There was something in that text; of that, I'm certain.

4

NOVA

Mack puts a plate of food down in front of me. The smell makes me instantly nauseous. I stare at it, but I'm struggling to focus. All I can see is the video of Kole being dragged from the bar by people with hoods over their faces. They zoomed in as they filmed it to show that he was breathing. Then, towering over him, one of them took a knife from their pocket and held it to his throat. They pressed the blade against his skin. A bead of blood broke free and trickled down his neck, tracing the ink of his tattoos until it disappeared into the neck of his shirt. I held my breath, hugging my stomach and squeezing the phone so hard the screen could have cracked. Then the video stopped, and a message appeared.

There's your proof, fire witch. Tell a living soul and you'll never see the Viking again. Sunset. Warehouse. Alone. We're watching you.

My fingers tighten around my phone. I have no idea how they knocked Kole out. He's huge, bigger than all of them and, apart from the nick on his neck, there were no signs of any injuries. The only way, surely, is if they drugged him.

I take a seat at the table, looking over at the others. For the first time, a kernel of doubt flits through my mind. My eyes land on Luther; his defined, sharp-edged profile. Square jaw, closely shaved head. Cords of thick muscle protruding from the sleeves of his navy-blue tee, rippling his rich ochre skin as he moves.

Sensing me looking at him, he catches my eyes. I look away quickly, heart thudding hard in my chest.

Someone is watching me. Could it be Luther? Could he be a spy?

Raising my coffee to my lips, I sip it shakily. It's lukewarm now, so I top it up even though I don't feel like drinking. I need to watch the video again. I need to study it for anything —the smallest thing—that might tell me who has taken him and what they want. I need to be alone.

"When did Kole say he'd be back?" Tanner asks as he sits down next to me. Setting his plate in front of him, he jabs at some bacon with his fork but doesn't lift it to his mouth.

I try not to stiffen at the mention of Kole's name.

"After his meeting." Luther slides into a seat opposite us and moves his gaze slowly from me to Tanner. I study his face for the smallest glimmer that might suggest he knows what happened to Kole and was part of it.

I'm still watching him when he exchanges a look with Mack that I can't interpret. In turn, Mack nods at Tanner. Something's going on here; I'm not the only one who isn't eating. Tanner is nudging food around his plate as if he's lost his appetite, Mack is staring into his coffee, and Luther hasn't even attempted to eat his.

Taking my hand, Tanner squeezes it. "Nova, there's something we need to tell you."

I'm not sure my brain can handle any more shocks. I press my lips together, bracing myself for whatever's coming.

"You're going to need to stay here at The Hollow for a while." He pauses, clearly trying to decide how to phrase what he's about to say next. "The bus driver who brought you to Phoenix Falls…"

"The bus driver?" I scroll back to my memories of the night I fled Ridgemore; I can barely recall his face.

Tanner nods. "He saw the video and recognized you." He lets the words sink in.

Leaning forward onto his elbows, Luther interrupts. "It won't be long before reporters start to arrive—"

"And police," Mack adds.

I let the news settle over me. "Magick or human?" All three guys narrow their eyes. "The police, will they be magick or human?" I meet Mack's deep brown eyes, searching for something that tells me he's got this under control.

He answers me without blinking. "Both." From across the table, he takes my other hand, the one Tanner isn't holding, and rubs his thumb across my knuckles. "Luther and I will speak to the Bureau. We'll keep you safe."

I look at Mack's hand, large and soft, curled around mine. Tanner has slid his arm around me. Luther is watching. Mack and Tanner trust him. I trust them. So, maybe doubting him is ridiculous. Maybe that's what they want—whoever has Kole. They want me to start panicking, pulling away from the mages who are trying to protect me.

I breathe out slowly. My chest is tight and hot, but although I know that my identity being blasted over national news channels is bad—very bad—it feels insignificant compared to Kole being taken.

I don't have room in my head to worry about it. All I want to do is get to The Cross and figure out what happened to Kole. I need to work out who has him, and what they want, and I only have until sunrise. Whatever the police—magick *or* human—want to do with me, it can't be worse than what will happen to Kole if I don't help him.

Pulling away from Mack and Tanner, I stand up and shake my hands at my sides. A spark flies from my fingers and floats across the room. Luther watches it, eyebrow arched, until it fizzles away.

"You think I'm safe here?" I ask, waving my arms.

"Of course, you're safe here," Tanner answers, barely missing a beat.

"Tanner, everyone in town knows I'm up here with you guys. They've seen me at Rev's, in The Cross, at the hospital. They've seen me with all of you. If someone comes looking for me, it'll take them all of five minutes to find me."

"So, we'll cast protection spells." Tanner pushes his chair back so hard it falls over then crosses the room in two strides and grabs my forearms. "Between the four of us, we have enough magick to seal this place tight so no one can get to you. Trust me, Nova." He runs his hands up to my shoulders and pulls me into his chest. I lean against him for a moment, listening to his heart beating. "Nothing will happen to you. I swear it."

"Tanner…" Mack is still seated, but his fingers are steepled together and he's pressing them against his chin. He's not looking at us, just staring out at the fountain. "Nova's right."

Tanner opens his mouth to respond but Mack shakes his head.

When he turns slowly in his chair, angling himself so he can meet Tanner's eyes, he says, "For now, she's not safe here. We need time to cast the spells and to figure out if the Bureau will help us or if we're on our own."

I untuck myself from Tanner's chin but don't move away from him. The feel of his breath moving slowly in and out is comforting.

Avoiding my question, Mack looks at Luther. "Can we use the cabin?"

Luther's lips tighten. A shadow crosses his face but then he nods. "Okay."

At that, Tanner seems to relax. His muscles untense and he rubs the spot in between my shoulder blades. "Alright." He smiles at me. "So, that's the plan. You'll hide out at Luther's cabin for a few days while we get this place secure."

"Cabin?" I ask, my mouth sandpaper dry at the thought of being whisked away from Phoenix Falls. "Alone?"

"No, no, not alone." Tanner swipes his soft, strong fingers across my collarbone and brushes my loose hair from my shoulder. "It's a few miles out of town, in the woods. No one knows about it." He breaks away from me and heads back to the table to shake Luther's hand. "Thank you. Seriously." The handshake turns into a hug.

"Like I said," Luther says gruffly, glancing at me over Tanner's shoulder, "you're my brother. She's your girl." Starting to grin, he shrugs and adds, "Plus, she's potentially the only being on Earth that can save us from the underworld rising up and swallowing us whole. So, we best keep her safe."

Mack and Tanner chuckle as Luther gets up, forks some food into his mouth, and ditches his plate in the sink. "We'll meet you up there when we've finished at the station." Catching me watching him, Luther stops. His head ticks to the side a little. A little stiffly, he says, "Nova, you'll be safe at the cabin. Tanner will make sure of it. Try not to worry."

"Well, that was uncharacteristically sensitive," Tanner quips, punching Luther lightly on the bicep.

In response, Luther simply rolls his eyes. But Tanner's right; for the first time, Luther seemed genuine in his concern for me. And the crackle in his voice when he said, *you're my brother, she's your girl*, has made me feel suddenly guilty for thinking he could have anything to do with what happened to Kole.

"Text Kole," Mack says to Tanner as he passes us, downing the last of his coffee. "Fill him in."

A spark of heat twitches in my palm. I clench my fist and hold it there. If Tanner texts Kole, and Kole doesn't reply, what then? He can't know Kole is gone. He can't suspect anything.

The heat in my palm flutters against my skin.

I will keep Kole safe. I will bring him back to us. I have to. I need him.

As Kole's face flashes in front of my eyes, the fire in my belly turns into something else; fury. White hot fury.

If they want me, fine, they can have me. But I hope they're prepared for what's coming.

5

KOLE

Eve is staring at me. She's painfully thin, her cheeks sunken, her eyes wide and shadowy. Small, black, spider veins snake out from the corners of her eyes. She couldn't look more like an F.H.B. addict if she had blood trickling from her mouth.

Which means two things: she's unpredictable and she's dangerous.

She licks her lower lip then moves to one side as the wolves haul me to my feet. I stumble as they pull me into the daylight. My eyes struggle to adjust.

Then we're in shadow again. They're shoving me through the doors of a large, empty warehouse. Concrete floor. Metal struts holding up a corrugated roof.

The wolves kick me to my knees then stand either side of the doors. Eve saunters in and skips a circle around me. The sound of heels on concrete makes her stop. Without speaking, she ducks into the shadows.

I refuse to look up from the ground. I know who I will see in front of me.

A long, lythe finger strokes my beard. A hand cups my chin then jerks my face upwards.

"Finally, *Ink Heart*. There you are." Kayla's face is barely an inch from mine. She licks her lower lip. Her scar, as I remembered it, is taut and angry. "Are you pleased to see me?" She ticks her head to the side. "I think you are."

Crouching down in front of me, Kayla puts her hand on my chest then traces a line downwards with her fingers. When she reaches my belt, I try to buck away from her, but I can't move.

She smiles. "Come, now, Kole, don't tell me you've forgotten how to play?"

I lift my head and look past her. I can see the van, parked at an angle. I search the ground beneath it. There, sticking up through the gravel… weeds.

"Ah, ah, *ahhh*.," Kayla takes her hand from my belt and waggles her index finger at me. "Naughty boy." She strokes the side of my face. "I know what you're thinking… your earth affinity is telling you to grow those tiny little weeds out there and strangle me with them. You're thinking you could escape and run back to your little fire witch."

Fire witch…

Kayla's eyes flash. A wolfish grin parts her lips. She stands up and paces in front of me. Her heels grind against the concrete. "That's right, Ink Heart, we know all about your little pet. But don't worry, we invited her to the party, and she'll be here *very* soon."

Before I can stop it, a thunderous roar escapes my chest. I meet her eyes, allow mine to darken, and let The Hunger and the fury rage inside me. I beat down the filth in my veins and fight through the haze until my magick begins to surge.

Kayla's eyes widen but she's not scared; she's excited.

She steps back, arms at her sides. The wolves run forward.

I roar again. Just as she said, the weeds spring from the earth. In seconds, they're like thick jungle vines, hurtling across the warehouse floor and knocking the wolves from their feet.

My vines grab them by the ankles. The older wolf shifts and, as his human leg turns canine, he jumps free. The younger one doesn't have as much control. He's reaching for a gun. Fucking pussy; resorting to human weapons.

I whip it out of his hands then wrap a vine around his throat. He paws at it, trying to break free.

I can't see the witch but it's not her I want to extinguish.

I fix my eyes on Kayla. She doesn't move. Even when vines creep up her legs, around her waist, around her throat; she stays stock still.

As I squeeze the breath from her, she smiles. "We know she's The Phoenix, Kole, and we have very special plans for her. If you kill me, Eve will kill you..."

Eve steps out of the shadows. My vision blurs. Eve flicks her wrist and a rod that looks like lightning flies from her palm, severing the vines.

Kayla unfurls herself and steps free. My strength is fading. The ground shifts beneath my knees. I've failed. That was my chance, and I blew it.

"And if you're dead..." Kayla's eyes widen as she draws a long, sharp fingernail across my throat. "Well, torturing your little fire bird won't be half as fun if you're not here to watch."

6

MACK

As we pull away from The Hollow, I put down the window and turn my face to catch the air. It smells different; there's trouble approaching.

"All right, Sheriff?" Luther asks, raising his eyebrows. He rarely uses my job title, and the formality doesn't sit well with me. "Sniffing out danger?"

I wrinkle my nose. Snow can smell a hole in a frozen lake from twenty miles away. His talent is muted by our human form but not extinguished completely. "'Fraid so." I drum my fingers on the outside of the door, letting my arm hang out of the window. The air is thick with tension. Bodies approaching. Reporters or cops, I can't tell. But neither one is good news.

Luther bites the inside of his cheek. He's about to turn on the radio when my cell rings. It's the station, so I put it on speaker.

"Sheriff, are you on your way?" The voice belongs to Daryl, a young recruit who seems permanently flustered.

"About five minutes out," I reply. "Everything okay?"

"You've seen the news?" Daryl clears his throat. "Deputy Ross called. He said you'd seen it."

"Yes." I pinch the bridge of my nose and look at Luther. We don't have time for this.

"Thing is, Sheriff, we've had ten phone calls about it already. Folks are scared the A.M.A. will retaliate. They want the witch gone. What do I tell them?"

As I click my tongue and search for a polite reply, Luther takes over, sensing I might be about to say something I later regret. "Daryl?"

"Deputy Ross, I'm sorry, I didn't know you were with the Sheriff. I mean, I guess I should have. You live together. It's just..." He trails off and exhales loudly. "Sorry."

"Daryl," Luther says, using his most tolerant tone, "if anyone calls, tell them we've got it under control. Tell them we're in discussion with the Bureau, and when we have concrete facts about the situation, the town will be updated. But, for now, there's no reason to think we're not perfectly safe."

"But the girl..." Daryl's tone has shifted. "The one in the video... she tried to kill a human. The guy she attacked was A.M.A. He had the tattoos and everything... until she burned them off him."

Luther rolls his tongue around the inside of his mouth. The rumor mill has already started turning. At least, as of yet, no one seems to have connected Nova with the four of us or The Hollow. But it won't take long; she's been out around town with Tanner, and she's been working at The Cross with Kole. Which means, soon, we'll have protesting townsfolk *and* reporters to deal with. A literal witch hunt.

"Daryl..." My voice comes out in a growl. "Law enforcement officers do not engage in gossip. All we know is that there was a fire, and a human was injured. Everything else is conjecture, speculation, and summation. There is no proof that the woman in the video was a witch. There's no proof she's here in town. We deal in facts. *Facts.*" I lean closer to the phone and bark, "Do you understand what I'm saying?"

"Yes, Sheriff. Sorry, Sheriff. Of course, Sheriff."

Before he can say anything else, I add, "We will be at the station soon. Can I trust you to handle things until we get there?"

Daryl offers another hurried, "Yes, Sheriff." Then I hang up.

The second I do, my phone beeps. "It's Tanner." I open the message and read it aloud. "Can't get hold of Kole. Can you drop by the bar and check on him?"

Luther makes a tutting sound with his tongue, clearly suspecting Tanner of being overly sensitive, but branches off the road that leads to the station and heads for The Cross instead.

When we arrive, there's no sign of Kole's bike, and the back door is locked, so we head around to the front. It's not yet midday. If Kole's inside, he'll be getting ready for opening. I try the door and, to my surprise, this one opens.

Inside, as my eyes adjust to the dim lighting, I scour the bar for signs Kole is here. I can smell him, but that doesn't mean much; it's his place, so his scent is woven into the fabric of it.

"Kole?" Luther calls out, stepping round a chair. He looks down as his feet crunch on something; broken glass. A chair at a strange angle. No sign of Kole.

Luther stops in a freeze-frame and conjures a fire ball into his palm.

There's a noise in the kitchen, from behind the double doors. A shadow crosses the small square windows in the top halves of the doors. Luther heads for one side, I head for the other. Before we reach them, they swing open and a tall, gangly frame backs into the room, pushing the doors open with their shoulders.

"Stop right there," Luther barks.

The vamp, because he's obviously a vamp, stops in his tracks.

"Turn around, slowly," I tell him.

He starts to spin around. He's holding a black plastic tray loaded with clean glasses. "Hey, fellas, woah..." He looks from me to Luther, takes in the flame in Luther's palm, and swallows hard.

I gesture to the bar. "Put the tray down, keep your hands where we can see them, and tell us what you're doing here."

The vamp nods hurriedly and does as he's told. Hands in the air, palms facing me, he stutters, "I'm Pete. A friend of Kole's? You might have seen me hanging out. I'm here a lot but I guess I don't stand out much." He's speaking quickly, eyes darting from me to Luther, which either means he's scared or hiding something.

I don't respond, just narrow my eyes and wait for him to finish explaining himself.

"We go to meetings together. He called and asked me to go with him to one this morning. He was in a bad way. Didn't tell me what happened."

Luther snuffs out the flame in his hand but strides forward and takes Pete by the collar. "Where is he?"

"He said he needed some space. Asked me to cover." Pete's eyes are wide, his cheeks sunken, as if he's purposefully sucking them in to sharpen his jaw bones. He's twitchy, and it's putting me on edge.

"Where did he *go*?" Luther asks, clenching his jaw.

"I swear, I don't know." Pete tugs at Luther's hands and Luther finally lets go. "All he said was that he needed some distance from this place and to tell you guys he'll be back when it's safe for him to be around *her*. He said you'd know what that meant." Pete looks at me and raises his eyebrows. "Do you know what that means?"

I don't reply, just nudge Luther and gesture to the door. "We should go."

Luther looks Pete up and down with suspicious eyes, but nods in agreement. "Tell us if you hear from him," he says sternly.

Pete mutters, "Sure. Of course. I'll call the station if I see him."

We're at the door when I turn and say, "Pete?"

He's behind the bar now and braces his hands on top of it as he meets my gaze across the room.

"What happened?" I gesture to the broken glass.

Pete blinks but answers fast. "No one cleared up last night. Merna quit. I wiped down all the tables but when I got to that one, I guess I wasn't looking. I knocked a glass flying. I was just about to clean it up when you guys arrived." He takes a cloth from beneath the bar and waves it at me.

I turn and leave without answering him.

Back in the car, Luther puts the key in the ignition but doesn't start the engine. "Did you buy that?" he asks.

"Not a fucking word," I reply. "Not the explanation for the glass. Not Kole taking off. None of it."

"Me neither." Luther pauses, brow furrowed. A wave of warmth tells me he's raging on the inside. "When I let Kole out of the cellar, he said he couldn't understand why he wasn't in worse shape. He expected to be high for days after tasting Nova's blood, but he was all right. He needed a meeting, but compared to how he was when she cut herself on the tattoo gun? He was fine."

"And even if he wasn't," I add, shaking my head, "there's no way he'd leave town. If he was that high, all he'd want would be Nova. To be close to her. Especially if Tanner's right about the blood bond."

Luther breathes out heavily and starts the engine. "So, then where the fuck is he? And why did that creep just lie through his teeth to a pair of cops?"

7

NOVA

"You don't need to take those..." Tanner slips his arms around my waist and snatches the clothes from my hands. "Didn't I tell you? There's a strict no-clothes policy at this cabin."

Despite the nerves rattling in my belly, I laugh and turn around. Slotting my fingers together at the back of his neck, I reach up and kiss him. "Is that so?" An involuntary tingle settles between my thighs at the thought of Tanner's unclothed body. For a moment, just a split second, I let myself imagine we're heading out of town for a romantic weekend. The kind where we'll spend all day in bed and watch the sun go down by the lake, a blanket around our shoulders and wine glasses in our hands.

"Oh yes, very strict rule." He runs his hands up beneath my shirt, his fingertips fluttering over my skin. A sigh escapes my lips. I return the gesture, sliding my hands down to his waistband and hooking my fingers inside it. He's not wearing boxers. I trace the tantalizing line of hair that starts at his belly button and thickens as it nears his crotch.

Tanner groans as my hand finds him. He presses into me and exhales a short, sharp sigh when I cup his balls.

There are too many hours until sunset. If I lose myself in Tanner, let him fill me up and pound the thoughts from my head, I might just survive the wait.

But as I tug at his jeans, he says, "Ah, Nova, stop…" and steps back.

I reach for him, to bring him back to me, but he takes my hands and squeezes them. "We need to get out of here." He smiles; the kind that makes his entire face light up. "But I promise I'll make it up to you."

"Do we really have to go?" I still haven't figured out how I'm going to get from the cabin to the warehouse. I found it on the map. It's just outside of town. From The Hollow it's only a twenty-minute walk. But from Luther's cabin? I've no idea where it is, but I'm guessing it'll be too far to walk. I also need to figure out how the heck I'm going to slip away without Tanner knowing. Because, of course, there's no question that I'm going. No matter what, even if it's a trap, I can't abandon Kole. I will not risk his life to save mine, and as the video hasn't given me any clues that might help me plot a way to get him back *without* doing what they say, I have only one option: Franklin Warehouse at sunset.

"'Fraid so." Tanner scoops up the clothes he took from me and deposits them into a large holdall. "Anything else you need?"

I shake my head. "That's all I have."

"Okay." Tanner brushes his lips across my forehead, stops to bite his lower lip, and says, "I can't believe I just stopped you when you had your hand in my pants," then opens the top drawer in his dresser, scoops out some clothes without looking at them, puts them in the bag beside mine, and nods. "Right. Let's get out of here."

***

As we follow the winding road that leads away from Phoenix Falls, I press my forehead to the cool of the window and watch the trees flit past. Light green merges with dark green until they're a haze of emerald, leaves indistinguishable from branches. The last time I traveled this road, it was pitch dark. I was scared, but hopeful.

Now, I'm just scared.

I've been in town less than two weeks. Yet, everything I know has been turned upside down more than once. I was a powerless human female in a suffocatingly toxic relationship. Then I was a witch who could create fire with her fingers. Now, I'm neither one of those things. I'm something bigger. *The Phoenix*. At least, after last night, the guys all seem to believe that's what I am. Whoever took Kole must believe it too, or why would they be trying to lure me to an abandoned warehouse?

Tanner's driving fast; as if he wants to reach the cabin as quickly as possible so we can finish what I started. We pass the junction that would take us to the warehouse. As we do, something crawls through me. Like a memory. A whisper of Kole.

He was here. He was close. It makes my whole body quiver. A sensation like vertigo sweeps through me.

I glance at Tanner. He's turned the radio on and is humming to it.

We've known each other for such a short time, yet I feel as if I could draw every inch of his face. The thought that this might be the last day I spend with him brings tears to my eyes. He smiles at me. "You okay?"

I nod and reach across to squeeze his thigh. "Just thinking how nice you are."

His brow furrows. Is he trying to read whether there's

something behind my words? "You're nice too." He lifts my hand and kisses it.

* * *

THE CABIN IS NESTLED SO FAR into the trees that it's barely visible until we're upon it. Shielded by towering pines, it's like something from a movie. There's a veranda that wraps around it, with steps out front, and a porch swing. I slot my hand into Tanner's and weave my fingers around his. "It's beautiful."

Tanner shrugs nonchalantly. "Yeah, Luther did a good job." He pulls our bags from the truck. "He built it with his own bare hands."

I raise my eyebrows in surprise. Tanner nods then gestures for me to follow him up the steps. Instead of unlocking the door with a key, he mutters something, and I hear a clunk that tells me a bolt has slid across.

"How does that work?" I ask.

"Luther cast the incantation. It has a code embedded in it. It's the same one we use at The Hollow."

"Like a password?"

"Pretty much." Tanner pushes the door and ushers me inside.

It's pitch dark, but Tanner moves to the windows and opens the shutters, throwing daylight into the room. I'm standing in the center, next to a large brown couch. It's covered with patchwork throws and terracotta cushions that make me want to curl into it and sleep for days.

Opposite the couch is a fireplace. On the other side of the room, a kitchen and a black old-fashioned stove. At the back of the cabin, directly in front of me, a huge picture window frames trees, a small jetty, and a gloriously blue lake.

"Luther *built* this place?" I walk toward the window, breathing in the silence.

Tanner nods. "I helped a little when I first came to town."

Suddenly, I'm picturing Luther and Tanner in nothing more than white vests and jeans, sporting tool belts, and glistening with sweat as they hammer and saw and chop. I bite my lower lip, force the image out of my head, and stop in front of the glass.

The view is breathtaking. The complete opposite of anything I ever saw or experienced in Ridgemore.

"Back home…" I pause, reluctant to bring my past into my present.

Tanner has deposited our bags on the couch and is beside me.

"Ridgemore is *not* like this." I release a long, slow breath and allow the motion of the air to release some of the tension in my shoulders. "When I was in foster care growing up, I used to dream about places like this."

Tanner brushes his fingers against mine. Then he utters the same incantation he used out front, and I realize the window isn't a window; it's a door. It slides back with ease, opening the inside of the cabin and allowing it to blend with the outside.

"Here." He takes a throw from the couch and hands it to me. "Go enjoy the view from the jetty. I've got some shielding spells to cast. Then I'll make us some tea."

"Shielding spells?" My stomach tightens. Spells to keep things out? Or to keep me in?

"To alert us if anyone's nearby." Tanner rubs my upper arm and leans in to kiss the spot below my ear. "When Mack and Luther get here, we can do something bigger."

I nod but, just as I'm about to step out onto the veranda, I stop and turn back to Tanner. "Mack and Luther?" I pause. "Kole's not coming?"

My stomach tightens and my breath catches in my chest; *I* know Kole's not coming, but Tanner shouldn't know that.

Tanner's expression changes. He winces a little as if he's annoyed with himself. "Shit, Nova. I didn't want to tell you."

My heart is hammering now. "Tell me what?"

"Luther and Mack stopped by the bar. Kole left a message for us." Tanner chews the inside of his cheek, searching for the right way to phrase what he's trying to tell me. "He needs a while to pull himself together. After last night." He moves closer, so close I can feel the heat of his chest against mine even though we're not touching.

"Last night?"

"Your blood. He went to a meeting, but he needs more time." Tanner meets my eyes and with feeling says, "It's not your fault. We needed to know about your past. Kole agreed. And he'll be okay. He just needs some space."

My mouth is sandpaper dry, and my tongue feels too big. Did Mack and Luther buy into that message? Or do they suspect something else is going on?

8

NOVA

I'm lost in the sunlight that's dancing on the surface of the lake. It's mesmerizing. There's a cool breeze, which softens the warmth of the sun. In Ridgemore, late summer hums with a thick, sticky heat. Here, it's kinder, and when the day inches toward night, a chill settles. But it's still a long time until sunset.

I take my eyes away from the water and look again at the map on my phone. A blue line shows the route from the cabin to Franklin Warehouse. Google Images tells me it's an abandoned, metal construction in the middle of nowhere.

Walking there would take me four hours, and Tanner would find me en route before I'd got more than a few miles away. Which means I need transport. I need his truck.

I put the phone away and wrap my arms around my waist, wondering what's been happening to Kole in the hours since they took him.

Whenever I think of him, the tattoo on my chest grows warmer. I raise my palm and press it to the spot where I can still feel my scar. Even though it's now hidden by ink, it will always be there. So will the memory of Kole's hands, his tongue, his eyes when they turned dark. The hunger that contorted his features. The fear that rocked through me as I ran from him.

"It's going to be okay, Nova." Tanner's voice surprises me; I didn't hear him coming.

He crouches down, swings one leg over the side of the jetty, letting his now-bare toes dip into the water, and angles himself toward me. When I don't reply, he looks out at the lake. I study his profile. He's ridiculously handsome. Smooth, perfect skin. The kind of hair you want to run your fingers through because you know it will be thick and soft, and delicious. Eyes that would make any girl want to bare her soul.

"We won't let anything happen to you." He's focused on the water and has pressed his lips together. "And whenever you're ready to talk about your family—what you saw in Kole's vision—I'm here.

"I know." I put my hand on top of his and trace the bumps of his knuckles. "I'm just…" I trail off. I don't know what to say to him that isn't a lie but isn't the truth either.

Turning to fix his eyes on mine, Tanner says, "Listen, you know I'm an empath, right?"

I nod silently.

"As a rule, I don't go snooping around in other peoples' heads. But a lot of the time, emotions kind of circulate like an aura around a person. And I see it, just like I see the color of your hair or the way you frown when you taste coffee without sugar."

I still don't speak. This is the part where he tells me he knows I'm hiding something. This is the part where I end up confessing and, quite possibly, ending Kole's life because I can't keep my mouth shut or my feelings to myself.

"What I'm trying to say is I know you're scared, and hurting, and I know there's something you want to tell me but can't."

I moisten my lips. My throat feels tight. "I'd tell you if I could," is all I can manage to say.

Tanner presses his forehead to mine. "You don't have to tell me anything you don't want to but—if it helps—I promise there's nothing you can say that will change the way I feel about you."

I rub my thighs and breathe out hard. "Tanner, I…"

Tanner dips his head. His gaze collides with mine. It almost takes my breath away. "If you're worried about what happened with Kole, don't be—"

My heart flips over in my chest. Even when I realize he's talking about the cellar and not the message, it continues to hammer against my ribcage.

"There's been something between you since you first saw each other." He tilts his head and smiles. "But I don't mind. In fact," He shrugs a little. "It's the opposite."

"The opposite?"

"I like it. I like *us*. The three of us. I mean, it was…" He breathes out a whoosh of air that makes his lips tremble. "I know how Kole makes me feel when he fucks me. I know what it's like to have my lips around his dick."

A shudder runs through me. Holy hell, if I needed a distraction, this is it.

Tanner leans in and snakes a hand around my waist, stroking the small of my back. With his lips close to my ear, he whispers, "I want you to feel that too. I want you to feel what I feel. I want to watch him torment you until you come."

I close my eyes but remain stock still. "What happened when I left you in the cellar? What did you do to him?"

Tanner reaches down, trails his fingers in the water, then brings them to my chest, circling the thin fabric of my sweater until the cold seeps through and dampens my nipple into a rock-hard peak. "Do you wish you'd stayed?" he asks, deliberately withholding his touch until I answer him.

"Yes." I lean forward, pressing myself into his palm, willing him to keep touching me, to make me feel so I can stop thinking. "I wish I'd let you fill me up. Both of you. I wish I'd given you my virgin ass while Kole took my pussy." A shiver runs down my spine. My clit throbs.

Tanner groans and his eyes flash with something mischievous. He dips his head and traces a line up my throat with the tip of his tongue. Cupping my face with his hands, he runs his thumbs over my cheeks then slots his fingers together at the back of my head and tugs so I'm looking at him. "I didn't know you had a filthy mouth, Little Star."

"There's a lot you don't know about me." I lick my lower lip.

Tanner winds his fingers into my hair. "Really?"

I nod.

"Do you want to know something about me?"

I nod again.

"I can hold my breath for a *very* long time."

"Hold your breath?"

Tanner flashes me an impish grin then, before I know what's happening, he's got his arms around my waist and he's pulling me into the lake.

As I sink beneath the water, the air rushes from my lungs. I can't breathe. The water is freezing cold. I move my arms, thrashing, reaching for the surface.

Tanner grabs my arms and turns me to him. The water is crystal clear. He's in front of me, his hair like a halo around his face. He pushes me up toward the light.

I emerge, gasping for air. He's still grinning. I slam my fists into his shoulders. "What the fuck, Tanner?! I can't swim! You know I can't swim!"

"I've got you." His arms are still around my waist. I want to keep punching him, but I stop because he's pushing us back toward the jetty.

"Why would you do that?" I ask, quieter, pushing my sopping wet hair from my face.

"Because now I can do this." Tanner takes my hand, kisses my palm, then lifts it toward the jetty. Something brushes my skin. I look up. He's winding a thin piece of rope around my wrist. "Do you trust me?" he asks, eyes fixed on mine.

I don't hesitate. Just nod.

He smiles, kisses me deep and hard, his tongue flicking out to meet mine, then winds the rope around my other wrist too, jerks them both up above my head, and binds me to the edge of the jetty so I'm suspended with my lower half in the water and my upper half exposed.

Tanner treads water, his eyes drinking me in. My thin white sweater has become translucent. The swell of my breasts and the ink of my tattoo press firmly against the wet fabric.

Meeting my eyes, Tanner says firmly, "If you want me to stop, say the word and I'll stop."

I nod. I have no idea what he's about to do, but whatever it is I know I won't stop him. I need him. I need this. My entire body is tight, waiting for him, fire crackling inside me ready to explode.

Before he disappears beneath the water, Tanner pulls off his shirt and throws it onto the jetty. His pants and boxers too. Droplets of water glisten on his chest. I want to lick them. I want to touch him. I tug on the rope, and he grins at me. Then he kisses me again, runs his hands down my throat, slots his fingers inside the neck of my sweater, and rips it open.

The force of the movement makes me gasp. Cold air hits my damp skin.

Without saying a word, Tanner pulls the cups of my bra down and eases my breasts free. They're exposed now, buoyed by the undulating water. I close my eyes, waiting for his warm tongue to flick across my desperate nipples.

But the warmth doesn't come.

When I open my eyes, Tanner is gone.

9

TANNER

Underwater, my eyes adjust to the lack of light and Nova's gloriously full hips come into focus. She's still wearing her jeans, but they're sodden and clinging to her skin. A shiver grips my dick at the anticipation of peeling them off her.

I can hold my breath for twenty-six minutes, but I won't need that long to make her come. To make her forget whatever's been tormenting her since breakfast this morning. To make her see stars.

I swim to her and place my hands firmly on her sides. Her stomach is soft, her skin pale. She feels even more delicious in the water. Somehow, still warm despite being lapped by the chill of the lake.

I unfasten her jeans and roll them down over her hips, taking her underwear with them. "Tanner..." She breathes my name. Her voice penetrates the water. My heart beats faster. I swim up her body and flick my hair from my eyes as I reach the surface.

"You want to stop?" I search her face, my hand reaching for the rope that's tying her to the jetty. Fuck, she looks amazing. Water nibbling at her tits, her nipples hard, the dusky pink circles around them dimpling with the cold.

A smile flutters across her lips. "No," she says.

A wave of desire hits me. Heat, electricity, fire. Her cheeks are flushed.

"I just didn't want you to let my pants float away. I only have one pair," she giggles. My chest swells; all morning, she's been fighting back tears but in this moment she's happy. She's laughing. She's my Nova again.

I grin at her and carefully place her clothes on the jetty next to my own.

"Thank you," she says, moving her shoulders in a way that makes her breasts tremble.

"May I continue?" I ask, my mouth close to her ear, as my hand travels down through the water.

She nods, holding her breath. She meets my eyes as I dip my head. I know she wants me to warm her breasts with my tongue, work her nipples, tease her with the heat from my mouth and the cold of the lake. I stop and look up at her. She tries to move closer, but the rope stops her. I grin and dive back under.

This time, I don't hesitate. I flip upside down, so I'm floating on my back beneath the water, and torpedo backward until my head is between her legs. Instinctively, she opens them to let me in.

I grip her thighs, palm her full, fuckable ass, and feel a shiver rock her body. She tries to move her cunt to my mouth, but I hold her still.

Tilting my chin up, I run a fingertip over her clit, barely touching her, then follow its movement with my tongue. The taste of her pussy blends with the feel of lake water in my mouth. I've never tasted anything so hedonistic.

I make slow, deliberate circles. I know she wants to grind

into me, force me to go harder and faster, but I won't. Not yet.

While I lap, lick, and suck her clit, she writhes her hips in the water, and the thought of her up there—exposed, helpless—makes my cock pulse with the urge to come.

If Kole were here, he'd tell me not to touch myself. He'd tell me to wait. So, instead of fisting my dick, I brace Nova's thigh with one hand and slide the other back further along her slit.

She quivers with anticipation. I dip a finger inside her cunt and collect some of the wetness. She's warm inside, like a hot spring. She clenches my finger, trying to keep it there, but I take it away and trace a long slow line to her ass.

She tenses a little. A flutter of nervousness settles in her muscles. She flinches as I touch her sweet, tight hole—the one she said no one had ever fucked. I pause, waiting for her to tell me to stop. Instead, she groans and tries to wriggle closer. The nerves are still there but she doesn't want to stop.

I send a plume of water to support her legs while I part her cheeks. She welcomes one finger, then two, eased by the soothing lake water and the juices from her pussy.

It takes every inch of willpower inside me not to add a third finger. To see how far I can stretch her.

Not too fast, Tanner. She hasn't done this before.

I know I need to be gentle, but my cock is desperate to take her, and my balls are pulsing so hard I feel like they might explode. I could untie her, throw her onto the decking and bend her over. But if she's going to let me be the first to fuck her like that, I want Kole to be there when I do it. I want his thick, Viking shaft inside her pussy when I ease into her from behind. I want to see her tits in his mouth, feel my balls slap against his as we fuck her in unison, rocking her back and forth.

That doesn't mean I have to stop playing though.

I take my tongue from her clit. She bucks and tries to find it again, but I slide backwards through the water and bury my face in her ass instead, swapping my fingers for my tongue.

She's moving too much. I need her still. So I grip her thighs and keep her above me. With my hands and my tongue occupied, I whip the water beneath her into a fast-moving cyclone and send it to her clit. She screams. A good scream. Her tits splash through the water as she writhes and pulls against her restraints. I send another vibrating cyclone of water to her clit, then another, creating my very own toy so I can please her cunt and her ass at the same time.

The water is heating up. Her body is coiled, ready to explode. She's close. Any second now...

"Tanner, stop..." Her voice is trembling. So are her thighs. "Tanner, please, stop."

I pull back from between her legs, right myself and swim to the surface. Running my hands up her sides, I find her cheeks flushed beet red, her hair hanging in bedraggled strands around her face. "Tanner..."

I search her face. All I feel is pure, hot, lust coming off her in waves. But she told me to stop.

"I need you to fuck me. Please fuck me."

A smile twitches on my lips. I kiss her deep and hard. When I pull back, her lips remain parted, and a small moan escapes them.

"Please. I need your dick inside me. *Please*."

"I like hearing you beg, Little Star."

She pulls at the rope, her elbows jutting out to the sides as she jerks forward.

I dip my head and take one perfect nipple between my teeth. I bite down, just a little. The pressure sends a lightning rod straight to my dick. I want to fuck her, too. But, more than that, I want to tease her. I want to keep her this way—

fizzing with the adrenaline that courses through her every time I touch her.

Something brushes against my dick. I frown. Her hands are still tied. Then I realize it's not her hands; it's her feet. She flashes me an impish grin and curls her toes around me.

Fucking hell, now that's something I'd never have expected to like.

I close my eyes. She moves her legs slowly through the water, pulling her knees up toward her chest as her feet keep hold of me. Then she stops, uses her toes to play with my balls, and wriggles so the water laps at her breasts.

I want to dive back under. I want to keep on teasing her until she cries with desperation. But I can't. My will power isn't that good.

I jump out of the water, untie the rope, and pull her up onto the jetty. We both stand there for a moment, dripping wet, the sun beating down on our naked bodies, taking each other in.

She's the most beautiful woman I've ever seen, or touched, or fucked. I almost don't want to move. Just want to drink in her curves, the way the sunlight caresses her hips, the swell of her glorious chest as she breathes.

"Where do you want me?" she asks, eyes wide.

My dick pulses hard. I take her hand. She sweeps her fingers through my hair and kisses me. Her lips are hot. Fiery hot.

I lead her down the jetty, not giving a shit that Mack and Luther could turn up at any moment and see us. Instead of going inside, I stop, push her hard against the nearest tree and spin her around.

She braces her upper arms on the tree and juts out her ass.

I smooth my hands over it. I'm so fucking tempted, but I

don't give in. I put my hands on her hips and pull her toward me. Then, without warning, I slam into her waiting cunt.

Nova lets out an animalistic cry and tips her head back. I wind her silvery hair around my fist and tug. She cries again. I tilt my hips, searching for the spot that will make her explode.

Beneath her touch, the bark of the tree begins to sizzle with heat. She's slamming back onto my cock. Again, again, again. Clenching tight. Squeezing me so hard I can barely take it.

My muscles tense. I shout her name and wrap an arm around her waist, pulling her into me.

I look up. A line of fire shoots up into the tree and her body dissolves into violent convulsions as she comes. The force of her orgasm squeezes one from me too. I lunge forward, almost losing my balance.

Nova stumbles backward. Still inside her, I hold on and wrap my arms around her. Her body is on fire. So is the tree. I pull a bead of moisture from her hair, make it swell, turn it into a stream, and send it up to put out the flames.

She watches, eyes wide, then laughs. "I guess we're a good team," she says, slipping her fingers between mine.

"I guess we are." I kiss her neck. She leans into me and then turns around.

"Tanner?"

I stroke her cheek with my index finger.

"Want to do it again?"

10

NOVA

After Tanner fucked me outside the cabin, I felt wild. Like electricity and fire and heat were swirling in my veins. Like, even though I'd just had one of the most earth-shattering orgasms of my life, I needed more. Another, and another, and another.

I watched him put out the flames I created, breathed in the scent of pine that filled the air, then asked him to fuck me again.

He didn't need to be asked twice.

He swept me into his arms, carried me inside, and made love to me on the couch. Then the kitchen table, then the bed upstairs.

Finally, exhausted, we fell asleep.

Except I didn't sleep. I pretended, closing my eyes and waiting until his breathing settled into a slow, steady rhythm. Then I sat up, pulled a sheet around myself, and went to the window.

Now, I'm waiting. Willing myself to have the courage to leave before he wakes up.

He's sprawled out on the bed, the sheet draped across his

lower half, toned leg sticking out, one arm above his head, and the other on his chest.

The sun is lower in the sky now. Its soft yellow glow makes his skin look buttery and delicious. Everything about him is beautiful. The way he makes me feel. The way he plays my body like a musician plays the cello; strumming exactly the right places and rhythms to make heavenly music vibrate inside me. The way he's strong and soft at the same time.

It's been just a few days since he told me he loved me. I didn't say it back. I wish I had, though, because if I never see him again after tonight, he'll never know what he gave me.

Finally, glancing at the time on my phone, I stand up and pace over to the bed. I don't touch him, just blow him a kiss and turn away.

Downstairs, I take fresh underwear, a tank top, and a plaid shirt from the bag that Tanner left near the door. I put them on, then look over to the picture window. My only pair of pants is still on the jetty. I pull open the door, as quietly as I can, and pad down toward the lake.

As I pass the scorched tree, a shudder runs through me. At the end of the jetty, I let the sheet drop and pick up my jeans and my sneakers. They're still damp, warmed by the sun but not dry enough to wear.

I tug them on, struggling against the tightness of the moisture. Like pulling on a used wetsuit.

The memory of Tanner's fingers catching on my skin as he peeled my jeans over my hips sends a spark of heat up my spine. I remember something Mack told me in our one and only magick lesson: "Your affinity is powered by your emotions. Use them. Latch onto them."

I focus on the heat and the memory. A small flame appears in my palm, but that's not what I want. I snuff it out and close my eyes. I try to remember the way it feels when Tanner's inside me and my body fills with heat. My skin grows warmer. I feel it building. When I touch my jeans, they're almost dry. A few more seconds, and they're back to normal.

I leave the sheet next to Tanner's clothes and go back to the kitchen. The keys to the truck are hanging on a hook by the sink. I lift them gently, making no sound. In the driver's seat, I stuff my phone into the holder on the dash and open the map showing Franklin Warehouse.

When I start the engine, I hold my breath. The truck rumbles to life. I wait, looking up at the cabin. There's no movement. It's not yet sunset, but the sky has changed color.

I reverse slowly, turn the truck around, then start down the dirt track that leads between the pine trees toward the main road.

At the end of the track, I stop, engine chortling, and tap out a text message.

Someone took Kole. They'll kill him if I don't go to them. They said to tell no one.

I'm sorry.

I love you.

Don't come after me. I'll be okay. I'm The Phoenix, remember?

I add a smiley face at the end. It seems ridiculously out of place, but I send it anyway. Then I drive away from him.

11

LUTHER

It's been one hell of a fucking day. From the moment we arrived at the station, we were fighting fires. No pun intended.

Panicked citizens. Cutthroat journalists, spreading gossip and swarming all over the town like a hoard of poisonous locusts, dripping venom in peoples' ears. Saying whatever they needed to say to get a headline or an exclusive scoop.

It wasn't even midday before someone told them they'd seen Nova in the bar. Gina, the water witch, if I had to guess.

On the one o'clock news, a blond reporter with red lips and spider-like eyelashes delighted in telling the camera, "In a shocking development, it seems the town's sheriff and his deputy are somehow involved in the conspiracy to hide the first witch to break the treaty. We now have multiple reports of her fraternizing with the sheriff and his friends. Some even suggest the witch has been living with the sheriff at his rather unusual mansion."

Now, driving away from the station, Mack looks so pale he's almost translucent. He managed to keep his cool when he watched the broadcast, but when the Bureau finally answered his call and told him he was relieved of duty until further notice, he flipped. He shifted in a heartbeat, let out an ear-splitting growl, and tore apart his own office.

Of course, when he barged out, I followed.

He shifted back when he reached the car and now he's sitting, stark naked, in the passenger seat.

"I'll stop by The Hollow. We'll lock it up then head for the cabin." I haven't asked what the Bureau said, but I can take a good guess.

"They don't give a shit," Mack grunts, as if he knew what I was thinking.

"About the reporters?"

"About the prophecy. All they're interested in is stopping a civil war from breaking out. Finding out whether Nova really did attack that weasel, Johnny."

I bite the inside of my cheek. Kole and Tanner have always been strong believers in the prophecy. Kole because he was the one who saw it, Tanner because he saw the lengths H.E.L. would go to in order to prevent it from happening.

Mack believes because he believes in *them*.

Me? I never bought it and, although I'm starting to change my mind, I'm not surprised that the Bureau is more focused on what's happening right now instead of what might happen at some indefinite point in the future.

Right now, humans and supers are perilously close to using Nova's little firework display as an excuse to slaughter one another.

"Apparently, they're sending a 'team' in the coming hours to investigate the situation," Mack huffs. "After all that we did for them, they wouldn't even listen when I spoke about the prophecy."

"Did you expect them to?"

Mack doesn't answer my question, just says, "Well, they'll

have to listen when they 'investigate' won't they? It's all connected. What she did to Johnny. What happened to her parents."

I let us settle into silence for a moment, and continue winding slowly toward The Hollow. Then I try to lighten the tone. "Does this mean Daryl is in charge until backup arrives?"

Mack shakes his head and smiles a wry smile. "I called Tanya and Jake. They're on their way in."

"Thank fuck for that." I drum my fingers on the steering wheel. We've reached The Hollow. "Want me to grab your stuff?" I ask. Mack nods. He's not in the mood for doing anything except brooding.

As I pass through the rooms of the mansion, gathering us each a change of clothes and our toothbrushes, I lock the doors and windows.

Back outside, Mack slides out of the car and pulls on the clothes I've tossed to him. Then together we add a layer of secondary lock incantations and an alarm.

"I'll drive." Mack stalks over to the driver's side and I don't argue.

We listen to shitty radio until it turns to the news. The blond reporter achieved what she wanted; her nasal speech is now being replayed on every TV channel and radio station in the country.

"What's worrying about this, Steve," the radio host says, "is that analysts are suggesting this seemingly small event could be the catalyst that sparks the country's next civil war. A war between supers and humans."

"Well, yes, Cherry. Some say it's a fight that's been a long time coming. Ever since supers came out of the shadows, tensions have been brewing—"

"Tensions?" I spit the word through gritted teeth. Humans burning supers at the stake, H.E.L. using black magick to torture and manipulate. That's not *tension*, it's *terrorism*.

"That's why representatives from both races—their government and ours—signed the treaty. To ensure humans felt safe and supers knew they needed to control their base instincts."

"A.M.A. piece of shit," Mack growls.

"But H.E.L. has been in existence for almost as long as the treaty and they've done terrible things to defenseless humans." Cherry's voice wavers as she amps up the drama for her listeners. "Why is this different, Steve?"

"Well…" Steve clears his throat. "Because, Cherry, this isn't some terrorist group. The Supernatural Defence Bureau themselves have, allegedly, been trying to take down H.E.L. for years—although we've yet to see much success on their part. But it isn't the actions of a sick-minded group of fascists we're talking about here. It's a normal, unthreatening, *witch*. A witch with no affiliation to H.E.L. who hid in plain sight and used her powers against her defenseless *human* boyfriend when she grew tired of him. Who attempted to burn him alive and make it look like an accident. Now, that's something very different. That's something that will leave every human in the United States of America asking, 'could I be next?'"

Mack punches the steering wheel and shakes his head.

I turn off the radio. We're nearing the cabin and sink into a tense, anxious silence. Then something clicks in my brain. "Shit…" I turn toward Mack.

He glances at me. "What?"

"The video—it's got to be the League who's behind it."

"H.E.L.? How would Nova's deadbeat A.M.A. ex get hooked up with H.E.L.?"

"Think about it…" My thoughts are moving quickly, everything slotting into place for the first time since the video appeared. "H.E.L. have known about the prophecy ever since Kole gave it to them. We know someone filmed the video taken outside Nova's apartment. What if the League already suspected she was The Phoenix? They've been watching, waiting for the prophecy to come true just like we have."

Mack breathes in slowly. Almost to himself, he says, "And when she sets fire to the apartment—"

"They convince Johnny to go on camera and they leak their video along with his victim speech. The A.M.A. is pissed and out for revenge. Reporters turn up in town. Supers want Nova gone. Humans want her punished." I wave my hands at the radio. "The whole fucking country goes nuts, starts talking about war and supers killing humans. They recruit more supers to their cause and, best of all, it serves as the perfect distraction. We're so busy running around town dealing with all of this that we forget about them."

"And everyone else is so busy chasing Nova, they don't notice that—Fuck!" Mack yells as he slams on the brakes.

I brace my hand on the roof of the car as it skids sideways and comes to a stop inches from what made Mack shout... Tanner.

Waving at us, leaning forward with his hands on his knees, he looks up through sweat-matted hair. I push the door open and stride over to him. Mack climbs out too and rushes to put a hand on Tanner's back, but I'm looking behind him, looking for Nova.

"She..." Tanner sucks in a shaky breath. "She's... gone."

"Gone?" Mack asks in a growl that's more Snow than him. "Gone where?"

When Tanner looks up, his eyes are filled with tears. His face contorted with emotion. "Someone took Kole. She's gone to get him back."

12

TANNER

I put my hand in my pocket and take out my phone. When I hand it to Mack, his eyes darken as if he knows what he sees next is going to be bad. Very bad.

He swipes open the screen but before he can finish reading, I'm already heading for the car. "Get in." I jump into the driver's seat. Usually, Luther would have my guts for driving his car but something about my tone must have told him to shut up and do as I say.

Mack climbs into the passenger seat and Luther into the back. They've barely closed their doors when I rev the engine, screech the car around, and make for the highway.

"Tanner, wait, do you know where she's going?" Mack hands the phone to Luther and leans forward to grip the dash. His knuckles whiten with the pressure.

"I have no idea. She snuck out and took the truck."

"When?" Luther's finished reading the message.

"I was sleeping. An hour ago, maybe." I swallow the lump in my throat that threatens to bring a tsunami of tears. "I knew she was hiding something. I should have looked deeper, but I thought..." I trail off. I thought she was scared of what was happening. I thought I'd helped ease her fear. I thought I'd filled her up with good feelings instead of bad ones.

Mack breathes in slowly. I can't work out if he's mad at me for failing to prevent this or just terrified of what she might have walked into. I'm not thinking straight enough to read anyone right now. "Nothing you can do now," he says. "Concentrate on driving." He glances over his shoulder at Luther. "Call your guys. Get them to trace Nova's phone."

Luther nods. I don't know who his 'guys' are, but he doesn't hesitate. In seconds, he's barking into the phone, "I need a trace. I'll text the number. No, I need it now." He hangs up, sends a text, then looks up at me in the rear-view mirror.

"Pull over. No point going any further until we know where we're going."

I hesitate but do as he says. When we stop, I catch Mack and Luther exchanging a meaningful glance.

"What?" I grip the wheel tighter, studying the pair of them.

"H.E.L.... this is what they wanted," Mack says. "Why the fuck didn't we see it?"

"See what?" I ask. Panic is coming off him in waves. Luther too.

"Releasing the video was just a distraction," Mack says.

"They know she's The Phoenix," Luther adds, turning to look out of the window at the darkening sky. "They couldn't take her because we were watching her. So, they took Kole and used him as leverage."

"They can't *know*." I'm clutching at straws. "We don't *know*, we just *think*."

"Well, then, they *think* she's The Phoenix." Mack is

growling now, and not even trying to disguise it. "And they got exactly what they wanted. We played into their hands. All of us. She's walking right into their trap."

13

NOVA

As I draw closer to the warehouse, my skin tingles. Like it's tightening over my bones. I can sense Kole; I'm getting nearer to him. I pull off the main road. It's been years since I drove— Johnny rarely let me take the truck—and I press too hard on the brake as I slow into the corner. It judders, matching the rhythm of my heartbeat.

I pass an old industrial complex. Large, ugly buildings that look out of place so close to the natural beauty of Phoenix Falls.

The GPS tells me to turn left. I indicate, even though there's nothing else on the road, and follow its instructions. The buildings I'm passing now look unused. Abandoned. Most are boarded up. Some have graffiti scrawled on their doors.

I take the truck down an alleyway between two short buildings. The GPS says I've arrived, but all I can see is a patch of scrubland. I stop the truck and get out. I look at my phone, squeeze it tight, and head toward the grass. I stop and look up at the sky. It's almost sunset. I shove the phone in my pocket and raise my palm. Am I strong enough to defend myself? I doubt it. But then I didn't think I'd be able to stop Johnny and look what happened; maybe all I need is a little pressure. Maybe when it counts, my power will surge to life, and I'll be back at the cabin in a few hours' time with Kole at my side.

Toward the edge of the scrubland, there's a line of trees. Examining them, I realize there's a break between them and what looks like a dirt track. I head for it, legs shaking.

My sneakers crunch on the gravel. It makes me hold my breath. As I walk, the sun dips lower in the sky. Finally, I see the warehouse. There's a small, black van out front. I pause beside it, watching the warehouse doors.

I stay like that for too many minutes. The sun inches lower in the sky, turning it a blueish-pink and then a blueish-gray.

If they're not going to come for me, I guess I'll have to go to them.

I approach the doors and knock. There's no answer. I push them and they swing open. Inside is cavernous and gloomy. I blink and shadows come into focus. There's something in the center of the room, curled on the concrete floor. A bulky silhouette which seems hardly to be moving.

I approach it slowly. A few paces inside, I realize what I'm looking at. "Kole," I breathe his name. The same invisible thread that pulled me to The Cross when I first arrived in town drags me into the belly of the warehouse. There's no one else here.

I run to him, my sneakers slapping the concrete floor.

"Kole," I say his name again. It makes my lips tingle.

He's hunched over. Crouched in a fetal position, in the same black t-shirt and jeans he wore last night. I kneel beside him and put my hand on his back. His shoulders twitch. He's breathing. Thank the stars, he's breathing.

"Kole…" I find the side of his face and stroke it, then tuck my fingers under his chin and tilt his face up to me.

He blinks into the dim light. "Nova?" His eyes widen. He sits up but doesn't move his arms. They're behind his back, his hands locked together as if they're tied with translucent chains. "Get out of here," he says, his voice husky like gravel. "Nova, go, now—"

"I'm not leaving you. I came to—"

Before I can finish, light floods the room. It blinds me. I grip Kole's shoulder. He yells at me to run but an animalistic rumble fills the warehouse, sending shivers through me. Wolves. Werewolves?

A figure appears. I position myself in front of Kole as if I somehow might be able to protect him. It's a woman. Tall, older than me, older than Kole. She has short dark hair and sharp, angular features. A large scar on her face. She smiles at me and tilts her head.

"Welcome, Fire Bird. I'm so glad you came to play with us."

My hand is on Kole's shoulder. Heat rushes to it but he looks up at me and catches my eyes. *No.* The word reverberates through me. *Not here.*

I blink at him. His lips aren't moving but it was his voice that filled me up.

I swallow down the heat. The woman nods into the shadows. Behind her, bright white eyes appear in the darkness. A snarl, a howl, then the wolves come for us.

14

LUTHER

The trace on Nova's phone tells us she's at Franklin Warehouse. While Tanner seems to genuinely believe we'll get there in time to rescue her, I know in my gut they'll be gone by the time we get there.

When we arrive, the warehouse is in complete darkness. I've only been here once, back when we first moved to town. Mack and I got wind of some F.H.B. dealers operating out of it. Turned out they'd set up a *Breaking Bad* style lab. We took them down, with more than a little help from Snow, and since then, Phoenix Falls has been a relatively F.H.B. free zone.

Then, the place was run down. Now, it's even worse.

Mack stops and crouches down. He clicks a light into his palm and waves it over the ground. A tangle of thick vines has erupted from below the cracked gravel.

Tanner mutters, "Kole," and follows the vines to the warehouse doors. They're closed. He moves to pull them open, but Mack stops him and points to his ear.

Nudging Tanner out of the way, Mack presses his ear to

the door. His bear hearing is twice as good as mine or Tanner's. He stands back and nods at me.

I pull a ball of fire into my palm, ready to throw it if I have to, and wait as he and Tanner yank back the doors.

When they open, Tanner stumbles backward. He clutches his head and lets out an anguished cry. When he opens his eyes, he runs inside, sending beams of light out from his palms to illuminate the insides of the building.

"They're gone!" He whirls around, desperately searching. "They're gone but I can feel them." He drops to his knees, muttering, "So much pain…"

Striding over to him, I crouch down and put my hands on his shoulders. "Either shut it out or use it to help us."

He's blinking through the pain, his eyes watery and wide.

"Shut it down or search for clues, don't let it overwhelm you, Tan. You know how. Come on." I meet his eyes and keep his gaze until he nods.

Shaking his arms at his sides, he tilts his head and closes his eyes. A million expressions cross his face, each lasting only a millisecond, making his features twitch and contort.

Mack is beside me. He's pointing at something on the floor nearby; a dark red stain. Blood. Next to it, is Nova's cell phone. Screen cracked. Abandoned. His nose wrinkles. Is that Nova's blood or Kole's? Either way, he's not going to tell me in front of Tanner.

"Fear. Pain. Disgust. Revulsion. Guilt." Tanner's words are short and sharp. "Fear. Power. Pain." His eyes spring open. "There's too much, I can't sift through it."

"Try." I'm still crouched in front of him. I glance at the blood and swallow hard. "You've done this before. Many times. Try."

Tanner nods slowly then closes his eyes again and leans forward to press both palms to the floor. "I can feel Kole. He was afraid and angry." Tanner's head tics to the side. "He felt powerless. Repulsed. Then…" Tanner opens his eyes. "A burst of anger. Like an explosion." He looks at the vines, severed, withering nearby. "I think he tried to fight back."

"And Nova?" Mack asks.

Tan stands up and folds his arms in front of his stomach. "She wasn't here as long as Kole was. There's less of her. Whispers of relief…" He swallows forcefully. "Perhaps when she first saw Kole. Then overwhelming fear."

"Pain?" I ask.

Tanner shakes his head. "I'm not sure."

Mack puts a firm hand on Tanner's shoulder and meets his gaze. "Do you feel anything that suggests she's dead?"

The word is thick on his tongue. *Dead*.

I might not get why the other three are infatuated with her, but the thought of Nova no longer being alive makes my stomach twist.

Mack pushes his hands through his salt and pepper hair—a trait all male bear shifters share and one that makes him look far more distinguished than he really is. A shiver runs through him, so violent it's visible in his shoulders and his forearms. He's changing. No matter how many times I witness a shift, it never stops being a head spin. But I can't look away. It's Snow's turn to be the detective now. "Let's go get our girl," is the last thing Mack says before his lips morph into a huge white snout with a shiny black nose.

I've barely blinked and there he is—Snow. The biggest fucking bear I've ever seen. Thick white fur and scary-ass teeth. Tanner puts his hand on Snow's shoulder. "Your nose is better than my brain. Go find her." Their eyes meet. "Take us to her."

Snow huffs out a cloud of hot air. Shakes himself from head to foot, then bolts from the warehouse.

Here we fucking go.

15

NOVA

Everything is dark. My eyes are open but it's like I'm wearing a blindfold; small whispers of brightness creeping through, telling me there is light somewhere just out of reach.

The floor beneath me is cool and smooth. I'm lying on my side, my right arm pressed hard against it. I try to move my hands to push myself up, but they won't budge from behind me. My feet won't either; my ankles are squeezed together as if they've been tied with something. I use my elbow—and a core strength I didn't know my stomach muscles possessed—to leverage myself into a kneeling position.

Through the darkness, Kole's voice finds me. "Nova, you're bleeding."

I turn in the direction of the sound. The tremor in his tone tells me he can smell my blood and is struggling to fight the pulse of hunger in his gut. But I'm not afraid of him. Even here, in the dark, I'm not afraid.

"You're bleeding," he repeats. "Are you alright?"

I scan my body. When the wolves came for me, I crouched, arms above my head, pressing myself into Kole's large chest. I felt him writhe from side to side, trying to throw them off with his shoulders. Until teeth sank into me, dragging me away from him.

"I'm okay." Wherever we are sounds large and empty. "Just a scratch." But as I speak, I wince because my collarbone is throbbing. My shirt feels wet, sticking to my skin. A tang in the air tells me it's blood. "Are you hurt?"

"Nothing that won't heal," Kole says, adding, "Fucking wolves."

I'm about to tell him to keep speaking so I can find him when the darkness begins to clear. As if I'm blinking ink from my eyes, the room comes into focus.

Immediately, I search for Kole. The second I find him, my wrists snap free from their invisible restraints and my arms lurch forward.

My ankles are free too. I stumble to my feet and rush to him.

At first, when I reach him, he flinches. His eyes are wide and almost totally black. A guttural noise vibrates in his throat. He blinks. He sees me. I know he sees me.

"Nova, you're hurt. I can't…" He looks away but I press my palm to the side of his face and bring his eyes back to me. His beard is thick and coarse beneath my fingertips. I don't think I've ever been this close to his face before. The swirl and groove of the tattoos on his face is hypnotizing. He shudders as I press my forehead to his.

"I thought I'd lost you. I thought they might have killed you," I whisper.

Kole's breath is coming fast and heavy. He leans into my touch. "You shouldn't have come."

When I sit back and meet his eyes, the darkness in his gaze seems to have faded a little. "I had to."

He watches me for a moment then nods. He feels it too. The bond we share that's now unbreakable.

I move to his side, run my hands down his arms, feeling the cords of muscle beneath my fingers. He's covered in cuts. Worse than mine. From claws and teeth.

When I reach his hands, I try to pull them apart, but they won't budge.

"Restraint spell. Powerful," he says. "The darkness was a blinding spell. I've never known a witch or mage who could do one."

"The woman in the warehouse? She's a witch?"

Kole's jaw twitches. There's a pulse in his neck that's beating hard and strong. "No. Kayla's a wolf. The witch is called Eve. I've never seen her before."

I sit back in front of him but don't take my hand away from his arm; I need to touch him. I need to be close. "But you've seen the wolf? Kayla?"

Kole looks away from me. I can't read his expression.

A beat of silence passes. His eyes graze the bloom of blood on my shirt then travel around the room, taking in our surroundings. He doesn't answer my question.

"Do you know where we are?" I ask, changing the subject and forcing myself to stand up and step away from him so I can pace the perimeter of our enclosure.

It's a large, empty room, made of what looks like marble. Floor to ceiling, there's nothing but smooth, shining gray stone. I can't see a door, and the only light is coming from warm yellow lamps—one on each wall.

"I think we're at their headquarters." Kole is still kneeling in the middle of the room, unable to move.

"Who's?" I ask, even though I'm sure I already know the answer.

Kole blinks at me. Every now and then, a wave of hunger seems to wash over him. His entire complexion darkens. His eyes become inky black pools. But then he fights it back, and he's Kole again.

"The Human Extinction League." As he speaks the words, he suddenly lurchers forward; the way I did. He pulls his arms around to his front, rubs his wrists, then staggers to his feet.

Without hesitating, he strides over and pulls me to him. His embrace is harder than Tanner's. Large, firm hands rove my body as if he's checking I'm really here in front of him. When he reaches my collarbone, he sucks in a sudden breath. His fingers brush the deep red stain on my shirt then he gently pulls on the neck and glowers down at my exposed skin. He swallows hard and examines the rest of my shoulder. "This needs cleaning and stitching." He steps back as if he's only just realized how close he allowed himself to become.

"If only Tanner were here," I say quietly. "He could fix both of us."

At that, Kole looks down at his own arms as if he's only just noticed he's injured too. There's a tear in the side of his black shirt, exposing a flash of bloodied skin. I gesture to it, and he winces as he touches it.

"We won't..." I pause. Kole looks at me. "We won't turn into werewolves, will we? From the bites?"

"Thankfully, no. It's not a full moon." Kole straightens up. His hair is long and loose. I'm not used to seeing it like this.

Starting to pace, he looks around the room.

"Are they watching us?" I ask. I can't see any cameras, but why would they leave us here, alone, unguarded?

"They're watching,.."

"Can you get us out of here?" I haven't been around mages very long, but I've seen some of their tricks and I've seen Kole's strength. Surely, there's something he can do.

Kole flexes his fingers. "They drugged me. There's something in my system. I can feel it."

"What kind of drug? F.H.B.?"

"No. F.H.B. makes me stronger. This makes me weak." A wry smile comes to his lips. "Human, almost. It took everything I had to try to escape from the warehouse." He shakes his head. "I shouldn't have done that. I should have waited."

"What do they want?"

"I don't know yet," Kole pauses. His eyes travel again to the blood stain on my shirt. They flash with blackness, and he takes the space between us in just a few strides. Without warning, he pulls me to him. He cups my face with his hand, weaves his fingers into my hair, and kisses me. It's a long, hard kiss. Hungry. Like he wants to devour me right here in this room. For the second time today, his voice appears in my head.

They want you. They'll test you—see what you can do before they decide whether to let you live.

His hands are on my back now, drawing me in. He's so close I can feel his heart throbbing against mine.

Show them a little. Don't let them think you're human or they'll kill you. But don't let them see the extent of your power. Control it. Control your emotions, no matter what happens, to buy us time so the others will find us.

The force of having his words inside my head brings tears to my eyes. I sink to the ground and Kole drops with me. Folding me into a tight embrace, he holds me as I cry into his chest. *I can't control it. Mack was going to teach me, but we didn't have the chance...*

Kole squeezes me tighter. *You have to. We need them to keep us alive. They'll only do that if they're not sure whether they're right about you.*

I take a few deep, heavy breaths and turn so my back is resting against Kole's chest. He loops his arms around my waist.

How can I hear you? I ask silently.

Blood bond. Kole sweeps my hair from my neck. I never

want him to stop touching me. *They can choke my powers, but they can't take that. It's unbreakable. But they can't know. They mustn't know, Nova.*

I sink back into him and close my eyes. The bite wound near my neck is hot and scratchy. I can't tell what time it is or how long we've been here. All I know is that I did what they asked, and they kept Kole alive. For now, we're safe. I just hope I can keep us that way. And I hope Tanner can forgive me for leaving him.

16

TANNER

We've been following Snow for almost an hour when he stops. We've reached the tunnel that leads through the mountain on the north side of town. Beyond it is Red Rock; the closest city to Phoenix Falls.

Snow stands in front of the tunnel's entrance, big white shoulders heaving up and down as he breathes. In the moonlight, his fur shimmers. He sniffs the air, tilting his nose up toward the night sky.

I look at Luther. He's moved into the driver's seat. I'm in no state to concentrate. I'm close to falling apart, and I know it.

When the guys first brought me back to Phoenix Falls with them, I was a shadow of what I am now. Nervous, jumpy, afraid. Perhaps that's why I felt so drawn to Nova when I first saw her in Kole's apartment—I recognized something of myself in her. Something of my past mirrored hers.

It took me a long time to pull myself together. Kole was a mess too. Over the past few years we've helped each other move on. We each have our way of coping. I bury myself in the depths of the lake and let the falls pound the pain from my body. Kole buries himself in the bar and in meetings. I give myself over to him, and he takes control of me. But there was still something missing. I wasn't quite whole until Nova.

If I lose her—if I lose them both—I'm not sure I'll be able to crawl my way back from the depths my grief will take me to.

"Tan," Luther says, reaching out to put a hand on my shoulder. "It's going to be okay. We'll find them."

I know he doesn't mean what he's saying. He thinks they're gone. For miles, Snow's been struggling to keep hold of their scent. Now, it seems like he might have lost it completely.

We watch as he paces back and forth in front of the tunnel. He's tired. When we first left the warehouse, he ran, full pelt. Now he's breathing heavily and his muscles are twitching.

Luther shuts off the engine and we get out of the car. When I put my hand on Snow's side, he's incredibly warm. Dangerously close to overheating from the exertion.

I search his aura. His feelings are usually easily distinguishable from Mack's. Even though they both represent half of a whole being, they're also separate. Symbiotic beings that live in the same body are very different from werewolves who are what they are no matter what form they take.

Right now, Snow and Mack's emotions are in sync. They're frustrated and afraid.

Snow dips his head and shakes it from side to side, huffing hard through his nostrils. He starts to shudder. His muscles twitch violently. I step back as fur smooths into muscle and his form shrinks. I blink and suddenly Mack is the one looking up at me, crouched, naked.

He stands, used to being exposed because every time he shifts, he shreds another set of clothes. Luther strides to the car, pulls out some spares from the trunk, and tosses them to him.

Mack's skin glistens with sweat and he's panting. He pulls on his clothes then scrapes his fingers through his hair, his eyes flashing amber as he lets out an exasperated sigh. "It's gone. Their scent. It stops here, like there's a wall of glass cutting it off."

"What if we go through the tunnel? It might re-emerge the other side?" Luther asks.

Mack shoves his hands into his pockets then takes them out and folds his arms, as if he isn't sure how to be comfortable. "It's gone. Erased. Not faded, just non-existent."

"So, a witch or a mage wiped it?" I ask, my stomach clenching.

Mack nods.

A wave of dread sweeps through me. Snow was our shot. The only other way for us to find them is if I...

"Tanner." Mack meets my eyes. "We're not there yet, okay? Let's go back to The Hollow. Talk it through. If there's any way we can avoid you having to jump, we will."

I wrap my arms around myself and pace away from him. Luther moves to follow me, but Mack holds him back. I pace to the edge of the road, lean onto my thighs, and heave into the bushes. I vomit until there's nothing left inside me. It leaves my legs so weak that I sink to the ground and put my head in my hands.

Now, Luther and Mack do come over. They help me up and we return to the car in silence. I climb into the back, leaving the two of them to talk in low voices up front as Luther turns the car around and heads back toward Phoenix Falls.

As we drive, I close my eyes. I know sleep is coming. I

know memories will come with it, but exhaustion wracks my body and I'm unable to resist.

I slide into the nightmare. The same one I had every night for years when I first came to Phoenix Falls.

I'm sitting on a bench in the middle of the university campus. The sun is shining, but it's cold out. I pull my jacket closer and look at the Halloween decorations strung up in front of the library. There's a party tonight. Mal will be there. My thoughts turn to what I'll wear then to whether I should bail and study instead.

I pick up my water bottle. It's almost empty, so I conjure it full and take a long swig. It cools my throat. I look at my watch, decide I could probably squeeze in an hour's study before the party to ease my guilt, stand and head for the library's entrance.

I'm a few paces away when my cell phone rings. "Tanner? Professor Raven. Can you come to my office? We need to talk about last week's assignment."

My stomach drops. Raven's class is the most difficult. My empathic talents far outweigh my elemental ones, and Raven's been riding my ass about water transfiguration for weeks; I can do ice, but can I get the hang of steam? Fuck no, and who needs to create steam, anyway?

"Now?" I ask too abruptly.

"Now," Raven snaps back.

Shoving my hands in my pockets, I trudge back across campus and into the wing of the main building that belongs to the water elementals. A large tapestry hangs in the hallway, stretching the entire length of the staircase. Opposite, a ten-foot-high waterfall runs down the wall. Instead of forming a pool that floods the stone hallway, it simply disappears.

I roll my eyes. Evaporation is another thing I struggle with.

Upstairs, Raven's door is open. He's sitting behind his desk, hands laced together. When I enter, he ticks his head to the side and the door closes. One of his favorite things to remind us of is the fact that moisture is everywhere. It's in the air we breathe, the ground we walk on. Therefore, we should be able to manipulate everything. Bend it to our will.

"Tanner, I think you know why you're here."

"Look, Professor. I know I suck, but it's not from lack of trying. I just..."

Raven narrows his eyes at me. They're dark blue, almost green, and his hair is slicked back with the-moon-knows-what kind of gel because it never moves, even when he does. "You just feel more 'passion' for your empathic traits?"

I pause, feeling as if this is a trick question, then nod. "Yeah. I do."

Raven sits back in his chair. To my surprise, a smile curls his lips. "Then you're going to like what comes next..."

17

KOLE

They keep the lights on all night and turn them off at daybreak. I know because that's what I used to do when I was with them—to disorientate our captives. While it's light, we sleep on opposite sides of the room. When it's dark, we find each other.

Nova's hands are like fire on my skin. The smell of her; the dried blood on her chest, the scent in her hair, the faint whisper of pine in her clothes send tendrils of hunger snaking through my veins.

But the blood bond has changed things.

A few days ago, a drop of her blood sent me over the edge. Now, I seem able to hold the hunger at bay. It's there, beneath the surface of my skin, itching like there ants are living inside me, but I can control it.

Nova curls herself into me. She's soft, and warm. If Tanner were here with her, he'd whisper loving things. He'd soothe her, hold her close. He'd know what to say to make her feel as if everything will be okay.

I've never been good at that.

I breathe out heavily. She takes my arm and pulls it

around her. She feels too small, and I feel too big. The curve of her ass is pressed against my crotch. My dick notices, despite the circumstances.

When I kissed her earlier, it was so I could talk to her without them realizing. If we'd have simply stood there, staring at each other, they'd have guessed; it would have taken all of a few minutes for them to realize we were bonded. Talking in voices no one else could hear. Better they think I just wanted her because of her bite wound and the blood.

But, fuck, it was hard to pull away.

Kole? Her voice fills my head.

I'm here. I don't move. My hand is resting on her stomach.

How long will they keep us in here?

I don't know. Maybe a day. Maybe two. It's what they do. They'll mess with our sleep, starve us, let us go thirsty. Weaken us in every way. Then start their games.

Nova shudders. The vibration of her body against mine is torture. *How do you know this? How did you know we're at their headquarters?*

My muscles tense. *I haven't been here before, but they had a similar room in the place they used when I was with them. That was a different life. It's-*

I know there are things you're not telling me. Nova slots her fingers through mine. *You can trust me. I want to know.* She turns around so she's facing me. I can't see her, but I can feel her chest rising and falling. I flinch as she slides her hand up under my shirt, fingers gliding over my abs. When she reaches my chest, she presses her palm to the spot right above my heart. *Trust me.*

I close my eyes, even though it's dark, and inhale slowly. *You know that Luther and I met at the Academy?*

I feel her nod.

He was always determined to join the Bureau. I wasn't. I was recruited.

And Mack was your professor?

Baloo. Yes. He was getting ready to leave the Bureau around the same time we graduated. He'd been asked to set up an undercover unit to investigate the activities of the Human Extinction League. There were rumors their power was growing, that there was something big in the works. So, Mack asked Luther and me to go with him.

And you said yes?

I sigh a little and rub my beard with my thumb and forefinger. How many times have I wondered whether the decision to join Mack's team was the wrong one? Too many to count. *I did. Luther's like a brother to me, and we'd grown close to Mack over our years at the Academy. He was...*

The dad?

I chuckle at that. *More like a big brother, but you can think of him that way if it makes you happy, Little Star.*

Nova smiles. I feel it in her breath and the way she moves her head. *It's the silver hair,* she says, *it makes him seem so much older. More distinguished than the rest of you.*

I roll my eyes and nudge her in the ribs. *He's not that much older. It's the bear in him. When male polars reach puberty, their hair turns white or silver.*

Really?

Really. I sigh. I want to get lost in this line of conversation. I want to talk to her like this; it's easy, and warm, and I haven't felt this way when talking to a woman for a very long time. But if I do, I'll never tell her the truth and she's right—she deserves to know what I'm holding back. *So, Luther and I graduated and the three of us spent two years gathering intel and preparing my cover. One day, we got word that the League was looking for a seer to help them access a prophecy. And that was my way in.*

How did you get them to trust you?

I'd build up a good backstory. Contacts who'd testify that I'd been at H.E.L. rallies, seen in the right places, with the right people, that sort of thing. Still, it took another two years for them to fully let me into the inner circle.

Nova's breath changes pace. *Was that how you met Kayla?*

I pull her closer and press my hands to her back. My fingers find her hair and stroke it a little. I hate thinking about Kayla with Nova in my arms. *She was the one who initiated me. I worked with her for eighteen months, proving myself. Test after test.* I swallow hard, praying Nova doesn't ask me what kind of tests. *I did bad things, Nova. Very bad things.*

To humans?

Yes.

But you had to... to make them trust you?

Yes.

Then I'm sorry for you. Her hand is still on my chest. She strokes me. By the stars and the moon, I want to let her take this pain away. The pain that's lived in me ever since I returned to Phoenix Falls.

Tanner and I do that for each other. We both know what it's like to do bad things for bad people because we don't have a choice, and our arrangement works. I need to feel in control and so does he. It's a game we play well. But it doesn't heal us. When we fuck, it's like a Band-Aid. A momentary release. But with Nova, it feels like she could truly make it better. For good. Like, if she could forgive me then maybe I could forgive myself.

But for her to do that, I'd have to tell her all of it. And I can't. Not here. Not yet.

So, I continue with what I can tell her. *The plan was for me to access the prophecy and distort it.*

You mean give them the wrong version?

Exactly. It's... complicated, the way it works, but I was good at what I did, Nova. I was powerful. I should have been able to deceive them without them ever knowing. Give the real prophecy to Mack and Luther, and the Bureau, then get out of there.

That's not what happened? She stops stroking me. Her chin is tilted up toward me as if she's trying to examine my face but can't.

Part of Kayla's initiation was to get me taking F.H.B. When mages take it, it sends our powers into overdrive. I was a powerful seer, but F.H.B. took me to a different level. I breathe in heavily. *I couldn't control myself. When it was finally time to access the prophecy, I gave it to them. All of it. Every word.*

Nova's body stiffens. I gave them the prophecy. I'm the reason they know she exists. *Then what happened?*

I left. The unit was shut down. I was too high to care. I was away for years. I only came back because of Tanner.

Tanner? Nova's heartbeat quickens. The way she thinks his name tells me that what exists between the two of them is almost as strong as the bond I share with her.

It's not my story to tell. He'll tell you when he's ready.

What if I don't see him again? Her question is so raw it makes my gut twist.

You will.

Her body shakes. I find her cheek and swipe my thumb over it. She's crying. When I kissed her before, it was filled with lust. This time, it's comfort I want to give her. I press my lips to hers. Her mouth opens, inviting my tongue inside.

18

NOVA

The way Kole's kissing me is different from the last time. It's a slow, deliberate kiss. His cock stiffens. I tilt my pelvis to press against it, and he releases a low groan into my mouth.

The floor is hard and cold beneath us. I don't know how long we'll be here. All I know is that my body needs him. Now.

I reach for his belt and unfasten it. He flinches and cups my hands between his, but I push him away and tug his jeans over his hips. I dip my head, searching for him with my mouth. When I find him, I run my tongue up the length of his cock. I curl my fingers around the base and squeeze hard. He's long and wide, so wide that my fingers scarcely meet when they're holding him. When I put him in my mouth, my lips have to stretch to let him inside.

His whole body is stiff, muscles coiled, primed to resist me but then his fingers weave into my hair and he holds my head still while he thrusts up. His salty tip hits the back of my throat.

Nova...

His thought dissolves before it's fully formed, the caress of my tongue taking his breath away. I stop and inch back up his body to find his mouth. I want him to taste himself, but before I can put my lips on his, he's tugging my shirt open and my bra down. His huge hands cup my breasts and press them together. He swirls his tongue around one nipple, then the other.

Lie down. Let me finish what I started in the red room...

I'm about to do as he says when a thunderclap of heat in my pussy makes me whisper, "No. Like this."

I pull down my pants and spin around. He understands what I'm doing. He tugs them off the rest of the way but leaves my underwear on and moves it to one side. I hook my arm back around his neck while he lifts my leg and then, holy stars, he's inside me. My gasp makes him stop. He holds me still, easing his width into me. Stretching my cunt until he's all the way in.

Everything about him is huge. His arms, his hands, his body. He's wrapped around me, squeezing me tight, keeping me exactly where he wants me.

As he starts to fuck me, I grab a fistful of his long, dark hair and tug. He groans loudly and grazes my neck with his teeth. A shiver of fear trickles down my spine. If he lost control right now, he could sink his teeth into me and lap at my blood and there would be nothing I could do to stop it.

Somehow, knowing that he could bite me sends a rush of fire through my veins. Every muscle inside me feels ready to explode. Tingling heat crawls up through my body. Kole shifts my hips. His tip finds the spot inside me that only Tanner has ever found. Thinking of Tanner sends me toward the edge. I slam back onto Kole's cock. The ground beneath us is hot, getting hotter. It starts to glow. I try to bite the sensation down. Not here. Not now.

Kole repeats the words. *Not here, Nova. Not now. Control it.*

I can't. Not while you're fucking me like this.

Smothering my thoughts, Kole lets out an animalistic growl and flips me so I'm pressed against the hot, hard floor. He pins my arms to the ground. I cry out, but he hooks his fingers in my mouth to quiet me. Keeping the scream inside makes me explode. I come in waves, shaking hard as I grind onto him, desperate for the sensation not to end. Sparks drift up through the air, tiny orange lights in the darkness. My hands are glowing with heat.

Nova... Kole leans down and growls into my ear. *Stop. Now.*

The tone of his voice sends a shiver through me.

That's an order.

I swallow hard, panting. I try to latch onto the heat. I picture the water Tanner threw on the tree. Hear the sizzle as the branches were put out.

It's working. The fire is fading.

Your turn. I can't see him through the darkness, but I can picture him towering above me.

Kole thrusts into me. Once, twice, three times. I feel him swell. Then he's gone. I let out a disappointed cry but then I hear him. He's fisting his cock. He's going to come on my ass.

He grunts hard. Hot cum lands between my cheeks. He falls forward, leaning over my back, breath heavy in my ear.

He stays that way for a long time. When his breathing slows, he lies down and drags me with him, so my head is on his chest.

Why did you do that? I wanted to feel you come inside me.

When I fill you up, I want to see your face, your body, all of you.

I curl my fingers around his hand. *All right. I'll wait.*

And then you can flame all you want. He moves his lips to brush the spot below my ear.

I'm sorry. I couldn't stop it.

He smooths his hand across his stomach. *Don't apologize. You did it. When I told you to stop, you controlled it.*

I guess I like you giving me orders.

I guess you do. His lips graze my forehead. Just a little. Then, he sits up. His hands find my bra and tug it back into place. He adjusts my shirt and helps me back into my pants. He's refastening his belt when he whispers in my head. *Were you thinking about Tanner?*

I sit up, legs crossed.

His name. I heard it. In your voice.

I stroke my hands up his arms and rub his shoulders. *When you moved my hips and found that... spot.*

Mmm. Kole's voice rumbles through my thoughts.

Tanner's the only one who's ever made me feel that good. So, I thought of him, then I thought of you, then I...

Kole takes my hand, he's standing up. He leads me through the darkness and when we reach the wall, he sits back down, leans against it, and positions me between his legs so I can rest my back on his chest. I tuck my knees up and Kole loops his arms around them.

"You know, they were probably watching us," he mumbles.

I blink into the darkness. "I don't care if they were... I could die here, and I couldn't die not knowing what it's like to fuck you."

Kole dips his head and kisses my shoulder.

And now I know, I'm even more determined not to die. I smile, even though he can't see me. *We're getting out of here, and when we're free, we're going to do that again. And again. And again.* I press my lips together and bite my lower lip. *I won't let them beat me. No matter what they do, I'll stay in control so Tanner can find us. We'll get out of here. I promise.*

Kole sighs and leans back against the wall. *I hope so, little star. I really hope so.*

19

KAYLA

The sniveling human smashes his fists against the glass then takes his cigarette and grinds it into the spot where his ex-girlfriend sits with Kole coiled around her like she thinks she's some kind of goddess.

"Why did you make me watch that?" he snaps, spinning around. With his burns still bandaged, he looks like a walking zombie.

"I made you watch because when she finds out, it'll make her angry, and hurt, and scared. And I need her to be all those things."

"Why?" Johnny takes out another cigarette, but I snatch it and toss it to the ground before he can light it. He tries to object but I snarl at him, and his eyes widen. After I told him about Nico, I realized I needed to make sure he didn't blab. Nico's relationship to me and the League has been kept secret since he was a cub. Letting it slip to an A.M.A. piece of filth was a mistake—the kind of mistake Ragnor would gut me for if he found out. So, as soon as we got Johnny away from the hospital, I showed him exactly what would happen if he crossed me and told my secret. Now, he's petrified of me. Which is exactly the way I like it.

"I need her to be full of feelings so that I can test her." I move closer to the glass. Kole must know that we're watching him, although our methods have evolved since he was with us. Back then, we had him and a few other less talented mages at our disposal. Now, we have Eve. The strongest, most powerful witch I've ever encountered. Eve knows many tricks. One of my favorites is her ability to make people see what she wants them to see. Right now, she's making Kole and Nova see stone instead of glass. So, they are oblivious to the fact that we've seen their vanilla little fuck.

Soon, we'll put her talents to better use.

From behind me, a shift in the air brings Ragnor's scent into the room. I whirl around. He strides in, chest puffed out, blond hair slicked back and tied at the base of his neck. He spots Johnny. In two strides, he's crossed the room and has his hand around his throat. As Johnny's face reddens, Ragnor turns to me and spits, "Why isn't this filthy human being drained?"

A whimper rattles in the back of my throat but I don't release it. I push my shoulders back and lift my chin. "He has a role to play, Ragnor. I have it under control."

Ragnor tightens his grip.

"We need him." I tip my head toward the glass. The fire witch seems to be sleeping. "If you want to torment her into showing us her powers, this disgusting excuse for a human is a crucial ingredient."

With a growl, Ragnor tosses Johnny to the ground. Johnny rubs frantically at his neck and scrambles toward the corner of the room where he cowers like a dog.

"How can she be the one we're looking for if she allowed this weasel to dominate her?" Ragnor looks from Johnny to

Nova. "You say he beat her? Cut her? Made her life a living hell?"

I nod, a smile twitching on my lips at the idea of the Fire Bird being made to sing. "Perhaps his cruelty released her power. Perhaps he can do it again."

Ragnor flexes his fingers, then clenches his fists. He was so certain that Nova was the one we were looking for. Now, he's starting to doubt himself. And that doesn't bode well for me. Especially given that *I'm* the one tasked with proving him right. "How long?" he snaps.

"One more day in the room. Then we'll start." I fix my eyes on his. "She's already shown she has abilities. We knew about the fire in the apartment, but I saw it with my own eyes. When Kole fucked her, she—"

He moves closer. "I don't want you wasting your time watching your long-lost pet and his witch. We need an answer. *He* needs an answer. We're running out of time."

"So, just tell him she's the one, kill her, and—"

Ragnor cuts off my words with a growl and squares up to me. "Do I need to remind you what will happen if we're wrong?" When he was certain, it was *I*. Now he's in doubt, it's *we*; so I'm equally responsible if it turns out we've simply picked up a human who's good at incantations.

I shake my head. I've heard Ragnor's speech so many times over the years that it's burned into my brain.

"The King must act when the planets align, which means we have thirty-six days to stop The Phoenix from rising." Ragnor grabs me and spins me around. He points at Nova. "If she isn't the one, we need to know. We cannot get this wrong."

"Ragnor," I say, wriggling back against him the way I used to when I wanted him to fuck me. "The others are watching their charges. None show the promise this one does. You said so yourself. And Kole believes she's the one. His friends back in town believe it. But if you want to be sure, why not just kill all three girls? Or give them to The King and let him decide."

"Because that was not what he instructed me to do." Ragnor runs his hands down my arms. He wants me. I can feel it. "And I need to see what she's capable of before I hand her over to Him."

He pushes me away, hard. At the door, he turns and says, "You have three days. Don't fuck this up, Kayla, or we'll all be sorry."

20

MACK

Luther stops the car outside The Cross. It's dark, which either means Pete the vamp locked up early, or that he never opened.

Tanner is still asleep in the back. He's been muttering, eyes flickering beneath their lids, since we left the tunnel. Whether he's dreaming of what has been or what will be, I don't know. But I know it's tormenting him.

"Take him home. I'll speak to Rev." I put my hand on the door.

Luther nods at me. "Careful, Sheriff."

I pat his back, climb out, and cross the street to Rev's store. Usually, this late, it would be in darkness, but there's a light on upstairs.

I knock and wait.

A curtain upstairs twitches. A few moments later, there are footsteps inside, and then the door opens, just a crack.

Rev's short black hair and large hooped earrings appear in the gap. She sees me and pulls me inside.

"Sheriff? Where the fuck have you been? Where are the

others?" She looks behind me into the street as if she's expecting to see Kole, Tanner, and Luther. "The town's gone mad. The entire *country's* gone mad." She sucks in her breath, shakes her head, then gestures to the back of the store.

Leading me past clothes and dressing rooms, she takes me up the small narrow stairs that lead to her apartment. It's dimly lit but the walls are painted a bright sunshine yellow. On the table, a silver teapot sits over a naked flame.

"I just made tea, do you want some?"

I nod, even though I feel like something stronger would do more to quell the seasick sensation in my gut.

As she pours, Rev says, "Is it true? What they're saying?"

"Which part?" I ask, taking an elongated silver cup from her and inhaling the smell of peppermint.

"The part about you *quitting* as Sheriff because you've been accused of hiding a fugitive?" She folds her arms, waiting for an answer.

I've known Rev a long time. She was the one who told me when The Hollow was put up for sale. She's younger than me, but we share a history with the place which means there's a level of trust between us. "No. I didn't quit. The Bureau removed me temporarily while they investigate what happened between Nova and Johnny."

"Did you tell them about the prophecy?"

I shake my head and almost laugh. "I tried. They weren't interested. But listen, Rev..." I put my tea down and start to pace. Snow is still seething with rage. Losing Nova's scent drove him wild and I'm struggling to stop another shift. "Kole's gone. He was taken. We think the League was behind the video leak. A distraction so they could get to him."

"They want him back?" Rev's eyes widen.

"I don't think so. I think they know about Nova. I think, somehow, they know that she and he have a connection."

She releases a slow breath. "Shit."

"They told her that if she didn't go to them, they'd kill him."

"So, she went?"

"Didn't tell us. Snuck out and took Tanner's truck."

"Fuck, he must be in pieces." Rev sits down hard in one of her kitchen chairs. "He's besotted with her."

I nod and sit down too. "Snow and I tried to track them but the scent has been masked." I hesitate, a pang of guilt tugging at my chest because I'm about to reveal something about Tanner I promised I would never tell a soul. But Luther and I discussed it; Rev is the only chance we've got if we're going to resist making Tanner jump.

"Tanner told you about Kole's past with the League, but did he tell you about his own?"

Rev cups her hands around her tea. She looks down into it. "I've seen glimpses over the years. A fleeting memory, here and there, but he keeps them under pretty tight guard."

I sigh and push my fingers through my hair. "Tanner's an empath. When he was at college, he struggled with his elemental affinity but excelled in his empathic talents. He was under the tuition of a professor called Raven, not far from graduating, when The League took him." I swallow hard, remembering the first time Tanner told me this story. "Raven was working for them. He had a theory that if a mage is deprived of their elemental affinity, their secondary talent will grow, magnify, become infinitely more powerful." I take a sip of tea because my mouth has become almost too dry to speak. "Raven noticed Tanner. Passed his information to the League. They knew he wouldn't willingly join up because he'd made no secret of hating them. So, they took him. They told him if he didn't do what they said, they'd kill his parents." I pause. "They're good at knowing how to persuade people to do what they want."

Rev closes her eyes. A tear escapes and rolls down her cheek.

"They kept him in the dark for years. Not a drop of water passed his lips. They hydrated him with a needle and a drip."

"Did it work?"

I nod solemnly. "It did, and as they'd lost Kole, Tanner became their new go-to mage for anything that involved torturing humans. He did things that he'll never forgive himself for."

Rev has wrapped her arms around her waist. She hugs herself tight and shakes her head.

"One of the things they taught him was how to jump. You've heard of it?"

A frown crinkles Rev's forehead. "When an empath jumps into another person's head?"

"More than that... when they transport their entire consciousness into another being. Take over their mind and therefore their body."

Rev visibly shivers. "That's dark magick, Mack."

"It is, and Tanner mastered it." I lean forward onto the table, resting on my forearms. "We need to get Nova back. Not just because Tanner is in love with her but because we believe she's The Phoenix."

"The girl destined to save the world?" Rev smiles a little and steeples her fingers together.

"Tanner could jump. He could latch onto her or Kole and find out where they are."

"But you don't want him to do that..."

"Not until we've exhausted every other option." I fix my gaze on Rev's. The same shadows that live in her eyes live in mine, which is why she's the only one we can ask for help. "Jumping blurs the lines between others' feelings and his own. It makes it harder for him to slam the gate closed when he doesn't want to feel. It..." I sigh. I don't have time to explain how broken Tanner's mind was when we first rescued him from H.E.L. "We want to try a locating spell, but we don't have Kole. We need a fourth."

I've barely finished speaking before Rev stands up, grabs her purse, and heads for the door. "You have your bike? Or am I driving?"

21

KOLE

Twenty-Four Hours Later

We've been in this room for over a day. The lights dip on and off. No food comes. No water. Nova sleeps and I wait. At first, she filled my head with her thoughts, asking me questions I tried not to answer. She wants to know me, and a large part of me wants her to. But I told her to save her energy.

She's sleeping with her head in my lap when the wall in front of us starts to shimmer. I shake her and she sits bolt upright.

"What's happening?" She grips my hand as the wall becomes a huge glass window with a glass door in its center.

Eve.

I knew she was powerful, but mirage spells— especially one that lasts as long as this one has—are a different matter altogether. Somehow, Eve has mastered restraints and incantations that usually take four mages to cast. I've never encountered a witch that powerful, even one who's taken as much F.H.B. as she clearly has.

Whatever is beyond the glass is in darkness, but I'm guessing it won't stay that way for long. I stand and help Nova up. She took off her sneakers hours ago. Her feet are now bare. They slap the cold marble floor as we back up toward the rear wall.

We wait. Her chest rises and falls as her breath quickens. *Remember what I told you. Control. Give them a little, not too much. Use your emotions, don't let your emotions use you.*

She doesn't reply, just squeezes my hand tight.

Finally, the door in front of us opens. But it's not Kayla who walks in. It's Eve.

"Hello, Fire Bird." She speaks in a sing-song voice as she sashays over to us. She smiles at Nova and plants a kiss on each cheek. "I'm sorry you've been waiting so long, but don't worry, the party's about to start." She slots her hand into Nova's and tugs gently. When Nova doesn't budge, Eve stops, turns slowly, and grins. "Come on, Fire Bird. We have to go take our seats."

"Seats?" Nova's voice trembles.

Eve's eyes land on me. She raises her eyebrows and looks me up and down. "I know Kole has already given you a private show, but what he's about to give us is going to be *so* much better. You really won't want to miss it." I watch as Eve's fingers tighten around Nova's fingers. Nova winces and attempts to pull away, but Eve jerks her arm up and says, "Ah, ah, ahhh. Play nice, Fire Bird. Or I might have to get very, *very* nasty. And we don't want that, do we?" She shakes her hair and laughs. "At least, not yet."

Eve tugs Nova again. This time, Nova complies. I try to lurch forward and catch her, but as I do, my legs are knocked from under me, and I end up on the ground. As my ankles slam together and the invisible ties return to my wrists, darkness descends.

I feel Nova moving further away from me.

I can do this if you can. They won't break me. I love you.

Her voice. She *loves* me? I want to see her. I need to see her. No one has ever said those words to me. No one.

I hear the door open and close. Her voice comes back, a whisper this time. *I love you. If I don't survive this, tell Tanner I love him too.*

22

NOVA

The witch who took me from Kole hums to herself. We're in an elevator traveling up. Four floors, six, ten. On the eleventh, it stops.

"How rude of me," she says as we wait for the doors to open. "I'm Eve." She extends her hand. When I don't shake it, she shrugs and shoves it into the pocket of her long billowy white dress. She looks like some kind of haunted bride. Her complexion is pale and gray around the edges. There are strange black veins at the corners of her eyes, and her fingers are adorned with so many silver rings that I can see just flashes of flesh between them.

"Don't be nervous," she says, grinning at me. "This is going to be fun."

When the doors open, daylight almost blinds me. It feels like the sun is directly in front of us.

Eve steps out of the elevator and pulls me with her. Immediately, I know we're not alone. As my eyes adjust, our surroundings come into focus, and I'm met by a huge crowd of people. Men and women.

"All wolves," Eve whispers in my ear. "You and I are the only witches. Isn't that neat?"

The werewolves are staring at me. They part as we approach, leaving a path down their middle.

I follow Eve down the aisle.

The werewolves make guttural noises as I pass. Their heat and their energy fizzes in the air. I look upwards. We must be on the roof of the building because all I can see is sky. There's a rose tint around the clouds that eases the throb of fear in my chest.

When we reach the front of the crowd, Eve points to a chair. It's almost like a throne. Large, made of wood, with a deep purple cushion on it. She gestures for me to sit down.

Silence descends. I expect her to chain me up, tie me down, do something to stop me from moving. But she doesn't. She simply stands to one side and says, "Ladies and gentlemen, distinguished members of the Human Extinction League, this is the moment you've been waiting for." She looks and me and tilts her head. "We're going to make the fire bird sing."

The crowd erupts into a flurry of whoops and cheers. They stomp the ground. The vibrations travel up through my bare feet and fear turns to terror in my veins. I grip the arms of the chair. Heat sizzles in my palms but I close my eyes and dampen it.

When I look up, the wolves have parted again. This time, the one Kole called Kayla strides toward me. She's tall, almost ethereal, but sharp-edged with eyes that make me shiver.

Behind her, with a chain around his neck, being dragged like a dog... Kole.

When she reaches the front of the crowd, Kayla gives the chain a jerk and Kole lurches forward. He fixes his eyes on me. They're dark and determined; he will not let them break him.

My body aches with the need to go to him, but I remain still, holding onto the chair's wooden arms.

Kayla brings Kole to the front of the crowd and positions him next to Eve. The werewolves watching are silent. Kayla drags a long sharp fingernail up Kole's throat, swirls it over the tattoos that spread up toward his face, and leans in close. "Kneel for me," she hisses.

Kole doesn't speak.

She scrapes her fingers through his beard. "Kneel for me," she repeats.

Kole still doesn't move.

Kayla flicks her eyes toward Eve. Instantly, Eve swipes her hand through the air. As if she's physically knocked his feet from under him, Kole drops to the floor. Kayla walks a slow circle around him then presses her shiny, high-heeled boot to the back of his neck and forces him his chest down.

Bent double, his head turned away from me, all I can see is the slight tremor in his shoulders as she grinds her foot in between them.

"Ink Heart has returned to us," she calls, waving her arms at the now-baying crowd. "And he brought a friend." She looks at me and the terror in my gut starts to twist and turn. "For too long, we have been searching for the one they call The Phoenix. For too long, she's evaded us. But now we believe we have her."

As Kayla speaks, Eve bobs up and down on the soles of her feet.

"So, turn her over then!" Someone shouts.

"Kill her!" Someone else cries.

I want to close my eyes, so I don't have to see the blood-lust in their faces, but I won't. If Kole can be strong, so can I.

Kayla waves her hands, and the noise dulls to a series of

whispers. "We will. But we need proof. *Absolute* proof that she's the one."

"What kind of proof?" a woman toward the front of the crowd asks.

"We need to see what she can do." Kayla turns to me. A slow smile stretches her lips. "But, of course, she's not going to show us willingly. So, we're going to have to... *provoke* her."

The woman who asked the question grins and rubs her hands together. Kayla steps aside, taking her foot from Kole's back, and nods at Eve, who takes center stage.

"Let the games begin!" she cries, clapping her hands.

As silence descends, Eve stoops down and cups her hand around the air as if she's gripping someone's throat. Kole lifts his head. Then his shoulders. Then his entire body rises and keeps rising until he's suspended in the air. His hands are still tied with invisible cord behind his back but his feet and legs dangle. His face reddens. The veins in his neck bulge beneath the chain that's looped around him.

Eve squeezes the air.

Kole starts to cough. He can't breathe. She's choking him, and I can't do anything!

The werewolves cheer.

As I watch, I try to slow my breathing. My skin feels hot and cold at the same time. The wooden arm beneath my hands is growing warmer.

Nova... don't... give them... too much. Kole's thoughts stutter into my head.

I blink at him, forcing myself to watch while, inside, I picture water and ice and cold winter mornings. Anything that might quell the heat that's rising in my veins.

Eve looks at me over her shoulder. She's still smiling. She drops her hand to her side and Kole falls to the floor. "Okay, fire bird," she says, "you want more?"

I don't answer her. Just watch as she tosses Kole, like a rag doll, across the rooftop. He slams into the concrete wall with a crunch that almost makes me cry out.

Looking up at Eve, he stares at her. His lips twist with determination. He will not give in. He won't show them his pain.

For what feels like hours but is only minutes, Eve toys with Kole. She rips his shirt from his body and twists his limbs until they look like they're about to break. She slams him to the floor; she chokes him again and again.

Then, finally, she stops.

My heart is hammering in my chest. My stomach is sick with heat. Fire trembles inside me, crackles against my ribs, licks the underside of my skin. Everything in my body wants to shower a volcano of rage down on the bitch who's torturing my mage. But I hold it in. Somehow, I hold it in.

Disappointed grumbles spread through the spectators—they weren't ready for the show to end.

Eve is breathless, her eyes shining. She calls through the crowd. "Andre, when you're ready my love."

There's a shuffling of feet. People move aside and two wolves appear. Literal wolves this time; like dogs but three times as large and with eyes that are far too human. One is large and silver, the other smaller and darker. A hooded figure trudges between them. A man. Skinny. Covered in bandages.

My breath catches in my throat. I'd know that frame anywhere.

Johnny.

When the wolves reach Eve, she strokes them each on the head. They sit down, one either side of Kayla, who's watching from the wings.

Eve takes Johnny's hand. She positions him in front of me, back to the crowd.

"Do you recognize him?" Eve asks me, giving his hood a gentle tug.

I don't answer her.

"Perhaps this will help." She pulls the hood from his head and grins.

Johnny stares at me. There's a gag covering his mouth. He can't speak, only look.

"You don't have anything to say to your boyfriend, Fire Bird?" Eve asks, smoothing her hands over Johnny's skinny, bandaged arms. "You don't want to apologize to him for what you did?"

"I have nothing to apologize for," I say, sitting up straight in my chair.

"Oh, I don't think that's true." Eve finds the end of the bandage and pulls it. Slowly, she unravels it, piece by piece.

Johnny is shaking. He winces as she peels the last of the bandage from his raw, mottled skin.

I take in the burns, every inch of them. I did that. *I* did that.

Spinning Johnny back around, Eve marches him over toward Kole. On his knees, my magnificent Viking looks up with disgust at my sniveling ex-boyfriend. If Kole wasn't restrained, he'd have his hands around Johnny's throat by now.

Eve crouches down to look into Kole's eyes. "How long have you been clean, Ink Heart?"

For the first time, a shadow of fear flickers over Kole's face. He is bruised, battered, and broken. But I know the thing that terrifies him the most is losing control.

Eve knows it too.

"How long since you tasted human blood?" She pulls Johnny down to the floor beside her and pushes him so he's inches away from Kole's face. "I could cut him open for you right now," she breathes.

Kole swallows hard.

Johnny tries to scramble backward and get away, but Eve flicks her hand and drags him back to her.

"Here?" She points to Johnny's throat. "Or here?" She lifts his wrist, sniffs it, then licks it. Then she shoves him away and nods at the wolves to retrieve him.

They grab an arm each and drag him over to Kayla. When they let go, he wraps his arms around his knees and starts to sob. I search for pity in my stomach but find none.

Eve reaches into her pocket. "Or how about some of the good stuff?" She's holding a small glass vial like the one I found in Kole's desk. She tilts it this way and that. The thick red liquid inside barely moves.

Kole's eyes have darkened. He tries to turn away, but Eve catches his face and brings it back to her. She unscrews the top of the vial. Kole's breath quickens. His shoulders shake. "It would make everything feel better," Eve says, stroking Kole's hair. "Just a taste. Hmm?" With one hand, she forces Kole's mouth open. With the other, she lifts the vial and tilts it. A drop of blood pools at the neck.

Nova. Give them... something. Do it. NOW.

Kole's voice rocks through me. I spring to my feet. "No!" I raise my hand.

Eve stops, tilts her head up at me, and widens her eyes. "Show me," she says, excitement quivering in her voice. "Show me your true self, Fire Bird, or your mage will remember what it's like to go to a very dark place." She has lowered the vial and taps it. "This? This is stronger than anything he's ever tasted. There will be no coming back..."

"All right." My breath rises and falls heavily in my chest. Hot, electric energy surges through me. "All right, I'll show you."

Eve stands up. Kayla walks toward me. Our spectators start to back away.

I lift my hand, stare at it, and release... a flutter of sparks.

There's a moment's silence then Kayla comes for me. She smacks my face, hard, with her open palm and I fall to the floor. "You think that's what we want to see?! We want to see what you can do. Not fucking party tricks a fifth grader could master!" She's about to kick me when Eve grabs her and pulls her back.

"I'm sorry... I can do better..." I murmur, hands over my stomach in case she thrusts her heel into me.

Kayla grabs the vial from Eve and strides toward Kole. She pinches his face and turns her eyes to me. "Show us. Now."

I wait for Kole to tell me what to do. I wait for his words. But they don't come. As I watch him, his eyes roll back in his head, and he slumps to the ground.

"Oops," says Eve. "Maybe I was a little heavy-handed. Ink Heart looks like he needs a rest."

Kayla stands up. She thrusts the vial back at Eve. "Have them taken to the cave. Wake him up. We start again at sunset."

Then she surges through the crowd and disappears.

23

TANNER

Rev has been up at The Hollow for over twenty-four hours. Between the four of us, we've tried every location spell we know, poured over books from Mack's library, and read incantations until our eyes were so sore we could barely keep them open.

And still, we've failed to find Nova.

Mack is asleep now. I'm amazed he lasted as long as he did after Snow's exertion last night. He's exhausted and snoring, which he only usually does if he's been drinking.

Luther is making coffee. Rev asks for hers black with no sugar. Usually, Luther might hit her with something smarmy like, "Because you're sweet enough, right?" But even he isn't in the mood for joking.

Rev yawns and rubs her face with her hands. The gesture smudges her eye makeup and leaves smoky black clouds like shadows on her cheeks.

When Luther brings over the coffee pot, we each take a mug and watch as it percolates.

I still feel nauseous. I woke from my dream in the car with a seasick sensation in my gut that hasn't shifted since. I might have given in to sleep before now if I hadn't been so desperate not to relive the rest of the nightmare.

"I need to swim," I announce, pushing the plunger even though the coffee hasn't had nearly long enough to brew.

"Go. We'll carry on here." Luther holds out his mug and I pour.

"Carry on with what?" Rev asks, raising her eyebrows defensively when Luther glares at her. "We've exhausted every option. We've tried everything. Unless you know a more powerful mage or witch who can help us…" She glances at Mack, slumped in a chair near the open door. "The Bureau has entire tracking teams, don't they? Surely, with your connections…"

Luther shakes his head. "Mack doesn't want to involve them until he knows whose side they're on."

Rev frowns.

I interject. "What Luther means is that, sure, the Bureau could help us find Nova. But what will they do with her when they do?"

"Ah." Rev lifts her coffee to her lips and sips it. "I hadn't considered that."

"We're on our own," I say, staring into my coffee. I know what I have to do, I just need to find the strength to do it. Looking up at Luther, I stand, down my coffee in one, and push my shoulders back. "I'm going for a swim. I need to clear my head. After that, we'll jump."

Luther doesn't object. We've all known, for hours now, that this was where we'd end up. We've just been putting it off.

"Are you sure, Tanner?" Rev asks. Hesitantly, she adds, "Mack told me about… what happened to you. Are you sure you want to revisit that side of yourself?"

I study her face. Has she seen something? Does she know

something that I don't? Will one more visit to darkness push me to a place I can't come back from?

"I'm sure." I glance at Mack. "Don't let him try to convince you there's another option. We all know there isn't, and I will *not* lose them because I'm too cowardly to do what needs to be done." I push my chair back under the table and nod at Luther. "Meet me at the falls in an hour. We'll do it there."

Luther sighs. A week ago, he'd have told us that Nova wasn't worth this trouble. Now, he's as certain as we are that she's The Phoenix and that she needs to be protected. He might not like her—or humans in general—but he likes demons even less. And he'd do anything in his power to stop the League and the nether realms from taking over.

BEFORE I LEAVE THE HOLLOW, I go to Nova's room—the room that became our room as soon as she moved in. From the dresser, I take her red halter top. The one she wore the first night we kissed—on the pool table. I hold it close to my chest, breathe in the memory of her scent, then take one last look at the bed and turn my back on it.

The drive to the lake is short. Ten minutes and I'm pulling onto the patch of dirt near the river. I abandon the truck and walk through the trees. The sound of the falls reverberates through the pines. Their raw, powerful energy sends a surge of adrenaline through my body. As I reach the water's edge, I pull off my clothes and leave them on the shoreline.

I wade in quickly, ice cold water slapping my thighs. The relief is almost instant. I dive under, trying not to think of the last time I did this—when Nova's body was suspended in front of me, mine to please and play with and taste. I swim down, down, down. The light fades. The water becomes murky. Weeds stretch up and stroke my stomach as I swim over them. Tendrils lap my legs, my ankles. Smooth as silk. I push up from the bottom and swim back up toward the surface but, before I reach it, I turn and torpedo back down.

I loop and dive and curl through the water until my lungs start to feel tight and force me up for air. Then I swim to the falls and stand beneath them. I let them pummel me. They will leave large, purple welts on my skin, but I don't care. I need this. I need to drown out the ache in my chest and remember.

I need to remember the things I did and how I did them, how I got to that place.

If I'm going to save them, I need to go back there.

I close my eyes.

I'm back in Raven's study. He's smiling at me across the desk. Then I'm somewhere else. A room. Dark. No sound. No water. Something breaks through the silence. Drip. Drip. I look down at my arm. A needle and an IV lead to a bag of clear liquid.

My lips are dry. I run my tongue over them. They're like sandpaper. Cracked. Parched. I try to ask for water, but no sound comes out, and no one comes.

For days no one comes.

For weeks no one comes.

By the time they do, I'm broken.

I snap my eyes open. Steely determination has settled in my belly. This is not the same. What I'm about to do is not what they made me do. This time, I'll be jumping to save a life, not help take one.

I leave the water and swim ashore. I stand beneath the early morning sun, letting it warm the droplets that run down my skin.

By the time the others arrive, I'm ready.

Mack is out of the woods first. He takes in my naked

form, picks up my clothes from the ground, and hands them to me. I nod at him and pull them back on.

Luther is behind him. I search for Rev, but Luther shakes his head. "She had to go. Someone looted the store. Apparently, she's been labeled a sympathizer because she knows us. They got The Cross too. She said she'd check in on it."

I screw my eyes shut. I can't feel anything else right now. I have to focus.

From my pocket, I pull out a black blindfold and hand it to Mack. "I need darkness," I tell him. "We'll go behind the falls."

Mack searches my face. He's afraid for me. It's coming off him in waves. I shut it down. I can't let it in.

I turn and head for the craggy path that leads from the shore, over the rocks, and disappears behind the waterfall. The others follow me.

It takes a moment for my eyes to adjust to the darkness. The cave is cold and wet. Water drips down the walls.

I head for the shallow pool at the back and sit on the floor beside it. Mack crouches in front of me. "Tanner, will this work? You said they deprived you of water to amplify your empathy. We're surrounded by it here." He looks at the curtain of fast-moving water at the front of the cave, the moisture on the walls, and the pool on the ground.

Luther is standing with his arms folded, watching.

"I'm hoping it might stop me from going too far. If I can stay tethered, it might…" I trail off.

Mack nods and puts a firm hand on my back.

I lift the blindfold. "I'm ready."

"What do you need us to do?" Luther steps forward but I raise my palm at him.

"If I'm gone too long, try to bring me back. Call my name. Remind me I need to find out where she is…" I pause and scrape my fingers through my hair. "It's hard to stay focussed when you've jumped."

Together, the two men I love as if they're brothers slide into the shadow. I turn away from them and fasten the blindfold over my eyes. I tie it tight and change my breathing. I slow it, don't allow my chest to fully inflate, don't allow enough air into my lungs.

Silently, I speak the incantation I know by heart and wish I didn't. Taken from a forbidden text, translated by worshipers of The King, and used by the League to further their domination of the human race. Used by me to save my parents from death.

Bae sra vuvar uk dordmakk, brems rar su ka.
Bae sra vuvar uk dordmakk, kruv ka sra voae.
Bae sra vuvar uk dordmakk, seqa ka rar kemd.
Bae sra vuvar uk dordmakk, ras ka em.

After just a few moments, my head starts to spin. I concentrate on the feeling, then I concentrate on Nova. I bring her to the forefront of my mind. Everything else is dark but she is the light. A beacon in the blackness. Shining. I latch onto her. She comes closer. I'm in front of her. I see her eyes. Two different colors. Pools of warmth pulling me to her. Her face is etched with worry. She's reaching out, but she's not reaching for me.

And then I'm not seeing her anymore. I'm seeing from inside her.

I'm feeling from inside her.

I am part of her.

When Nova moves her head, I feel as if I'm swimming underwater. As if I'm looking through her eyes but I'm far away and nothing is solid. Everything moves. Shimmers as she turns her head.

There is no sunlight where she is. It's dark, only small slivers of natural light coming from somewhere above.

At first, I wonder whether my brain has merged our realities because the place she's in is so like the place I'm in. Like the cave behind the falls, Nova is somewhere cold and wet. She shudders as she walks slowly around it, running her fingers over the slick walls.

She stops, wraps her arms around herself, and breathes heavily, swallowing down a sob.

From behind her, a voice says, "Nova..."

She whirls around. The movement is fast and almost knocks me off balance. The room sways in front of my eyes as she rushes forward.

Through watery eyes, she blinks. In front of her, something comes into focus. A cage. A large, metal cage. She grabs the bars and tugs at them. *Kole... you're okay. I'm here. I didn't let them see. I controlled it.*

I hear her words but they're not coming from her lips.

Then I hear his. *You did good, Little Star. You did good.*

They can hear each other. How? I feel the swell of pride in Nova's chest as he says those words to her.

Come here. Let me see you, she tells him.

He's at the back of the cage. Only his enormous frame is visible. My own relief merges with Nova's. He's alive. He's okay.

But when he staggers forward, the force of her anguish makes me cry out. Blood drips from his forehead. His eye is swollen. His hands are black and blue. He clutches his side. He's not wearing a shirt and a huge purple bruise blooms over his ribcage.

Here. Come here. She reaches for him, sliding her fingers through the bars, but before he can get to her, he wavers and falls.

Nova kneels down, unbuttons her shirt, and slips it off. She starts a fire, a small one, and warms the shirt. Urgency courses through her. She passes the shirt to him. "I don't have anything for the cuts, but the warmth might soothe them."

Nova. Don't... his voice is strong, commanding.

I'm not showing them anything they don't know I can do. She inches closer to the bars and holds them tight, peering in at him as he presses the warm fabric to his side.

"Tanner... Tanner..." A different voice breaks through the haze of Nova's thoughts. Mack's voice. "Where is she, Tanner? Find out where she is."

I search Nova's mind, but there's nothing to tell me where they're keeping her. I scrutinize the slices of her surroundings that I can see through the corners of her eyes. Nothing. Then a noise behind her makes her spin around.

Someone enters. A man. Tall and skinny. He throws something at her. A bottle of water. She stands and tries to speak but he's already turning away.

This is my shot. I have to take it. I don't have the chance to look at Kole one more time. I just focus on the man in front of me and repeat the incantation.

There's a rush of air, a spinning sensation that makes me feel as if I'm floating. And then I'm not inside Nova anymore. I'm inside a werewolf.

24

NOVA

"I fucked up." I move as close to the bars as I can and loop my fingers through them. "I didn't know what to do. I didn't know how much to show them."

"You didn't fuck up." Kole presses against the bars closest to me. "You gave them just enough."

"Kayla said they're starting again at sunset..." I trail off. Icicles of dread prickle my skin. "Kole, what if they make you drink?"

"I can handle it." He winces as he talks. "I've done it before."

"But..." I grip the bars. My breath is shaky. "I don't want to lose you."

Kole meets my gaze. "You won't." He shuffles closer and his fingertips find mine. "I can handle it."

I want to believe him, but I know he's scared. He glances at my hand. The wound in the center of my palm has nearly healed but I know he's thinking about the red room.

"Nova, after I tasted your blood, I thought I'd be..." He sucks in a sharp breath as if pain has just gripped him. "I thought it would take me days to come down. But I think the blood bond changed things. I feel different around you now. The hunger's still there but I can control it."

I absorb what he's saying and press my lips together.

"You don't believe me?" He squeezes my hand.

"Of course, I do. It's just…" I try to move closer. I want to touch him but with the bars between us I can only manage the lightest brush of my fingertips against his skin. "Kole, you might have been able to control the hunger you feel for *me*, but what if it's not my blood you're tasting? What happens then? Eve said the stuff in that vial was more powerful than anything you've had before."

Kole grunts a little and turns himself so he's facing me instead of looking at me sideways. "Nova–"

"You said you disappeared for five years after you accessed the prophecy… I can't lose you for that long." I find his hand and hook the top of my finger around one of his. *I meant what I said. I love you.*

Kole closes his eyes. When he opens them, they're moist and wide. He shakes his head. *Your safety is the most important thing, and you mustn't think about me. About us. What you're destined for is bigger than that, Nova.*

I sit up, kneeling, and press myself against the bars. *Fated to five… that's what the prophecy says. Do you really believe you're not one of the five? The way we both felt when I arrived in town. A blood bond when I've never tasted your blood. The things you do to my body…*

Kole's eyes roam my face then dip to my chest, my stomach, my hips. He drinks me in for a moment then says, *If I am one of the five, then maybe it's meant to be this way. Maybe I'm meant to sacrifice myself so you can get out of here.*

Before I can answer him, he reaches out and brushes his finger against my chest. It grazes my nipple. I don't want to give in. I want to make him promise we'll fight them together. That we won't let them infect his mind with that *stuff*. But my body responds too well to his touch.

"I'm in a lot of pain," he says, tracing a slow circle over the parts of my breast he can reach.

"Don't change the subject."

"This could be our last few hours together."

"Then we need a plan."

"What I *need* is a distraction." He moves his hand down and uses the tip of his finger to tweak the top of my jeans. "Dance for me…" A smile curves his lips.

Heat crackles in my chest and turns into a quiet laugh. "You're half dead and you want a striptease?"

"What better time for one?" Kole looks down at his bruised torso. "I really am in a lot of pain, Little Star."

I shake my head at him. *Now*, of all times, he decides to get a sense of humor? "As you're the one in the cage, I think you should be the one doing the dancing." I reach for my back pocket. "I'm sure I have some dollar bills in here somewhere, and you do have a very cute ass."

Kole chuckles a deep throaty laugh that makes him grab his side and breathe out a heavy rush of air. "Tanner thinks so," he answers, looking up at me and enjoying the flush of pink that colors my cheeks.

For a moment, we both laugh. As it fades, I stand up and step back from the bars. I tug at the hem of my tank top and pull it up over my head.

Kole looks at me as if I'm a fucking goddess. It sends instant warmth to my upper thighs. "Nova, I didn't mean it. You don't have to…"

"I can't do anything else to make you feel better." I unfasten my jeans and slide them down. "But I can do this."

"There's no music." He takes in the swell of my hips, my stomach, my thighs.

"I'm not planning on dancing." I reach back and unhook

my bra. As it drops to the ground, Kole releases a throaty, rumbling sound that makes me wish his tongue was vibrating on my skin.

Never in my life have I stood, butt naked, in front of a man before. Not willingly. But the look on Kole's face fills me with something... I feel powerful. I feel beautiful. And I don't care that we're in a damp cave and that we're quite likely going to be tortured again in a few hours' time.

If anything, the knowledge that pain might be coming makes me even more desperate to feel something else.

Tell me about Tanner. I lick my finger and lower it to gently stroke my nipple.

Kole tilts his head. With one hand, he grips the bars. With the other, he adjusts his cock. *What do you want to know?*

Tell me what it's like to fuck him. Tell me what you do to him.

Breathing out, Kole licks his lower lip. As I slide a hand to my pussy and find my clit, he answers me. *He likes it when I take control.*

I'm wet already. I start slow deliberate circles around my clit.

When I need a release, we meet. Usually by the lake. I tell him to wait for me. He swims then sits by the falls, dripping wet, naked, until I get to him.

I change my pace. Apply a little pressure that makes me moan.

Sometimes, he wears a plug. So, he's ready for me.

I squeeze my breasts with one hand and circle my clit faster with the other.

He's very good at sucking my dick. He can take my whole length in his mouth. It makes his eyes water, but he does it. Like the good boy he is.

I run my hands through my hair and tilt my head back. Trickles of electricity spread down my legs and up my sides.

Come here. Kole moves his head closer to the bars. *I want to taste you.*

I take my hand from my cunt and give him my fingers. He licks them slowly then sucks at them. I finger-fuck his mouth, moving them in and out, faster, harder.

He tries to reach me through the cage, but his hands are too large, they won't fit through. I press myself against them and give him my nipples. Those, he can reach. With his tongue, he laps and sucks and bites. Not too hard. But hard enough to make me slam forward and beg for more.

Give me your panties. He looks at where they lie on the floor.

I pick them up and pass them through the bars.

Kole presses them to his face and inhales deeply, then he stands, pulling himself up using the cage as leverage.

He unfastens his pants and pulls out his cock. It's hard and huge. Pre-cum glistens on its dark red tip. I desperately want to lick it from him.

Sit down. Open your legs. I want to see you fuck yourself. I want you to come for me.

I do as he says. I sit on the cold, damp floor and spread myself for him. Towering above me, he wraps my panties around his dick and starts to rub them up and down his length, moving his palm over his slit and then down. Squeezing, then up again.

I lie back, draw my knees as high as I can, and slide two fingers into my pussy. My walls clench, wishing it was Kole's thickness filling me up. I press my palm to my clit, then move my other hand to my breasts and toy with my nipples.

Come for me, Little Star. Show me how you'll come when Tanner's in your ass and I'm in your cunt.

I curl my fingers inside myself, leave my nipples, and play harder with my clit. A moan escapes my lips. I move my hips, swirling my fingers inside myself, applying pressure until I'm ready to detonate.

Come with me. I look up at Kole. My walls flutter but I hold the orgasm back. Hold it. Hold it. *Come with me, Kole.*

He jerks forward, slams his arm into the bars, fists his erection faster and harder. He's still using my underwear. The friction makes him groan. His cum fills my panties. Some of it escapes and dribbles down his fist. Watching him, I explode. A cry leaves my mouth. I arch my back against the floor. My whole body is shaking.

I lie there for a moment, panting as the waves crash over me. I hear Kole's breath, heavy and fast.

I look up at him as he slides down the bars of the cage and leans against them. My panties are in his hand. He looks at them and says, "I'm not sure you want these back."

I stand, legs trembling, and extend my hand. He passes them to me. "Actually, I do." I pull them on and slide them up my legs over my hips. Kole's cum settles next to my own wetness.

His mouth falls open a little. "Fuck," he breathes and rattles the cage. "Fuck," he says again.

I put on the rest of my clothes then move closer. He brings his face to me so I can stroke his beard. *If they make you drink that stuff, and you get close to me, you'll smell yourself on me. You'll smell your cum, and mine, and maybe you'll remember the way back.*

The lust in Kole's eyes turns to something warmer. "Nova..."

I lie down on the floor next to his cage and reach up to hook my fingers around his. "Do you feel better?" I ask.

Kole laughs a little and squeezes the part of my fingers he can reach. "Almost forgot we were facing certain death," he quips.

"Me too." I close my eyes, focussing on the warmth and the tingle in my muscles. "Me too."

25

KAYLA

"Were we wrong about her?" I storm toward Eve with a force that would make anyone else flinch. Eve simply smiles.

"We weren't wrong, she's just stronger than we thought." She strokes the mahogany dining table that's positioned in the center of the room. Above it, a large chandelier clinks as a breeze whips through the open window.

"Stronger? All she managed to conjure was a light that wouldn't even spark a bonfire on Halloween."

"She's controlling it." Eve shudders and runs her hands down her lithe body. "I can feel it." She tosses her dark hair over her shoulders and licks her lower lip, hopping up to sit on the table and swing her legs back and forth. "We just need to give her a little more to get worked up about." She looks to the corner of the room where Johnny sits staring vacantly into the aether. Eve jumps down from the table and sidles over to him. Crouching, she tweaks her finger under his chin and says, "Don't worry, puppy, Mommy will make you feel better soon."

Johnny stares at her, frozen, eyes wide. His red raw scars

glisten in the moonlight that streams through the window. Eve trails a long finger down the side of his face and stops at his throat. She strokes the place where his veins are biggest. I know what she's going to do before she does it; I've seen it many times before.

Fixing her eyes on Johnny's, she bends down, lifts her long billowy dress, and takes a knife from her boot. Before Johnny realizes what's happening, she has the knife at his throat and she's making an incision. Not big enough to kill him, just big enough to start the blood flowing.

She turns and grins at me. I roll my eyes. "Fine. Not too much. Now we're done with him, I want him drained. I'm not wasting good product."

Eve's eyes sparkle.

Johnny seems unable to move. Only his eyes dart back and forth as blood pools in the crease between his neck and his shoulder. Eve dips her finger in it, raises it to her lips, and sucks. A tear escapes Johnny's eye and rolls down his cheek to merge with the blood. Eve tilts her head, lowers her mouth, and laps at the knife wound. As she drinks, she becomes more frenzied, more hungry, more desperate. She grabs his shoulders and straddles him. She writhes in his lap, grinding against him as she has her fill. Even though his blood hasn't been fermented yet, it still gives her a kick.

Finally, I bark, "Enough."

She whirls around, her eyes dark. The black veins at the corners of her eyes stretch out toward the edges of her face. Blood stains her chin. She makes a noise that's almost a snarl.

But when Johnny passes out and goes limp beneath her, she stops, wipes her hands on his shirt, and stands up.

He slumps sideways onto the floor.

"Shit, Eve. He's bleeding too much." I take my cell from my pocket and dial Andre. "Eve's overdone it, the human needs to be drained before we lose a thousand dollars' worth of perfectly good blood. We're in the dining room."

When I hang up, Eve is staring at the ceiling. "Aren't the stars beautiful?" she asks, blinking at the chandelier.

I put my hand on her shoulder and spin her to face me. I'm about to tell her to pull herself together when Andre hurries into the room. He's brought two others with him, whose names I don't care to remember. They haul Johnny to his feet and drag him toward the elevator.

"When you're done, don't finish him." Eve turns to them, smiling, and walks over to cup Johnny's face. "I want to play a little more."

Andre looks at me for confirmation. I nod. If there's one thing I'm sure of right now, it's that we need to keep Eve happy.

Behind Andre, the elevator doors open. But it's not empty. Ragnor is inside.

I glance at Eve. Her eyes are wide. She's drinking him in as if he's a god. His gaze passes me over and lands on her instead. He looks her up and down, takes in the blood on her chin, the blackness of her eyes, and laughs. "I'm glad you're having fun, Eve," he says as he strides into the room.

She runs to him like an excited child. "I really *am*," she says, smoothing her hands over his chest.

Ragnor stands stock still and lets her touch him. He's at least a foot taller than her and three times as bulky. But while Eve's diminutive frame might be easily snappable, he knows she has power. Which means, deep down, he despises her. He despises any woman with strength.

When Eve starts to get carried away, Ragnor takes her by the wrists and says, "I need to speak to Kayla alone. Why don't you go and *please* yourself with one of the boys?"

Eve wrinkles her nose and stretches up to whisper in

Ragnor's ear, "You mean you don't want to play with me, Master?"

Ragnor's throat twitches. His cock too, probably.

Eve slides her hand down his chest, finds his belt, and snaps it open. Ragnor doesn't move. He lets her put her hand down his pants and grip him hard. She looks at me over her shoulder. "Maybe Kayla should join us?"

I meet Ragnor's eyes. I've often thought that if he remembered how good we were together, he might find his way back to me. But he looks away, wraps his fingers around Eve's wrist and tugs her hand free. Holding her tight with one hand, he refastens his belt with the other. "Not today, Eve." He lets go and nods in the direction of the elevator. "Now, go. Get your fill elsewhere. I need to speak to Kayla."

Shrugging, Eve saunters into the elevator and waves as the doors close.

"She's a liability," Ragnor growls as soon as she's gone.

"She's loyal to The King and to us." I pull a chair out from the table and sit down. Ragnor stands for a moment then sits opposite me. The move is unexpected. I anticipated him yelling, throwing things, getting me by the throat and threatening to tear me apart because I haven't got an answer yet.

Instead, he leans onto his forearms and laces his fingers together.

"Tonight, you torture the girl?"

I nod. "I hoped seeing her mage humiliated would be enough to make her show her power, but Eve says she's controlling it."

"So, we need to increase the pressure." Ragnor sits back and nods. "What do you plan?"

"Eve has some tricks up her sleeve."

"I have another." Ragnor's lips stretch into a grin. It sends a shiver through me. "In fact, I have something very special for our fire witch." He takes his cell from his pocket and lifts it to his ear. "We're ready. Come on up."

We wait in silence as the elevator ticks back up the floors. When it reaches us, Ragnor stands and walks over to it.

The doors slide open. The second they do, my heart leaps into my throat. I spring to my feet and take the space between the table and the elevator in just a few paces.

"Nico?!" My son's beautiful face brightens into a broad smile when he sees me. I throw my arms around him and squeeze. "You didn't tell me you were coming..." I kiss his cheek. He hugs me back then pulls away.

Ragnor thumps him on the shoulder. "Welcome, son. It's been too long."

My eyes narrow and my heart starts to thud; Ragnor only ever acknowledges Nico as his son when he wants something. Not a single person knows that Nico is the product of mine and Ragnor's brief union.

"Father," Nico says, nodding politely.

"Come. Sit." Ragnor gestures to the table and walks Nico over to it with his arm around his shoulders. When we sit down, Ragnor takes a chair beside Nico.

Dread settles in my stomach.

"Why is Nico here, Ragnor? You've always said he should stay away from this place. Maintain his cover." I lace my fingers together and grip hard, trying not to let fear make my voice tremble. "Even Eve doesn't know about his connection to the League."

"And it will stay that way." Ragnor stands and moves to the head of the table. "But the time has come for Nico to do more than enjoy a lavish celebrity lifestyle while schmoozing the rich and famous, and making verbose speeches."

"It's a little more than that, Father. I report back to you on—"

Ragnor bares his teeth and cuts Nico off mid-sentence.

Nico slides back in his chair and looks down at the table.

"The time has come for you to prove your allegiance through more worthy actions." Ragnor puts his palms on the table and leans forward. Staring at Nico, he says, "Everyone else in this building has risked their life more than once for the cause. Now, it's your turn."

I reach for Nico's hand across the table. He takes it. "What do you want him to do, Ragnor?" My voice trembles.

"I want him to do what he's good at – I want him to take on an acting role."

A brief shadow of relief washes over Nico's face.

"He's been playing the role of do-gooder celebrity super for long enough. This shouldn't be too much of a stretch."

Nico takes his hands back from me and straightens up, trying to look confident. "What is it you need me to do?"

Ragnor smiles and takes out his phone. Sliding it to Nico, he shows him a picture of Nova. Nico tilts his head as he looks at it. "Isn't she the girl from the news? The witch who tried to kill her boyfriend?"

Ragnor nods. "We believe this girl is The Phoenix. When she was five years old, her human parents brought home a foster brother. His name was Sam."

Ragnor's expression doesn't change as he says Sam's name, but it makes my stomach constrict.

"He was a werewolf cub, placed into the human foster system because no one knew of his heritage. One day, little Sam bit Nova. Nova got very angry. So angry she started a fire with nothing but her bare hands."

Nico is still studying Nova's picture. "So, she's not human but her parents were?"

"That's what we're trying to figure out," I mumble.

"She killed her parents and her brother in that fire." Ragnor is smiling now. "But we're going to give her a gift."

Nico looks up at his father.

"We're going to make her believe that Sam is alive, and that all these years he's been wandering around not knowing who he is." Ragnor leans closer to Nico. "We're going to make her believe that *you*, my son, are her long-lost darling brother."

As Nico's mouth opens to ask a question, Ragnor adds, "You share an uncanny resemblance. He even had a birthmark like yours." Nico looks down at his hand and the small bird-shaped mark that has graced it since he was born.

"Like mine?" He frowns.

I look away. Tears are biting at my throat. I want to plead with Ragnor, beat my hands on his chest, to beg him not to use our son for whatever he's got planned. But I know it would be futile. If anything, it would only fuel his desire to make it happen.

"There are just two things you'll need to do..." Ragnor taps the table. "First, you'll need to memorize your backstory. Second, you'll need to change your appearance."

"My appearance? I thought you said I looked like him?" Nico swipes his fingers through his thick black hair.

"You do, but if Sam had survived the fire..." Ragnor stops and looks at me.

I shake my head. "No, Ragnor. No."

"If Sam had survived the fire, he'd have scars to prove it." Ragnor fixes his eyes on Nico and says, "Are you willing to go through a little pain for the good of the League, son?"

Nico swallows hard and presses his lips together.

I can't sit any longer. I spring to my feet and tug at Ragnor's arm. "Ragnor, no. Surely, there's another way. Eve can make the fire witch *see* the scars. It doesn't have to be real."

"Oh, but it does. Because if something were to happen to Eve, Nico's cover would be blown." Ragnor picks up his cell. "But we will need her to help them heal. They need to look like old scars, not fresh ones." He swipes the screen then says,

"Eve? When you're done, we need you. Meet me in the control room."

I'm still gripping his arm. "Ragnor, let me try my way first. We could break her without ever having to involve Nico."

Ragnor cups my face with his hand and squeezes. With his other hand, one by one, he prises my fingers away from him, then shoves me back into my seat. "Unfortunately, Kayla, you've failed to do what I needed you to do. You had your chance. I'm done waiting." He looks from me to Nico.

We hold hands across the table.

He gestures for Nico to stand. "Son? Let's get you to hair and makeup. Finally, you're about to secure a starring role."

26

LUTHER

Finally, the jump is over. Tanner's eyes roll in his head, and he falls backward. Mack drops and pulls him onto his lap. He coughs, spluttering, then turns his head and vomits hard into the small pool of water next to him.

Mack helps him sit up. He's drenched in sweat and trembling.

"What happened? You seemed to be coming out of it then you went back under." I crouch down next to Mack, Tanner's excruciatingly pale face making me want to pull him into an embrace. He shakes his head and pushes Mack away, stumbling to his feet.

"I'll tell you as we walk," he says, but as he speaks his legs waver, and he reaches out to brace himself on the wall of the cave.

Mack and I slot his arms around our shoulders and all but carry him out of the cave.

When we reach the car, we deposit him in the back and hand him a bottle of water. He takes a long slow sip. "Head for the tunnel," he says, looking at Mack. "I know where to go from there."

"She showed you where she is?" I ask, leaning on the seat as I turn to look at Tanner.

"She's underground. With Kole. He's injured. Badly. He's in some kind of cage."

My muscles tense. Rage swells in my gut. They hurt my brother? I'll fucking kill them.

"But Nova doesn't know where they're keeping her, so I had to jump again."

"Again?" Mack's fingers flex on the steering wheel as he and I exchange a worried glance. "I didn't know that was possible…"

"I've done it before." Tanner grips his head as if the car is spinning for him. "A werewolf brought her water. It was the quickest jump I've ever done but it was worth it." The hint of a smile twitches his lips. "He showed me a lot, that wolf."

"He showed you where they are?"

Tanner nods. "He took an elevator to the sixth floor. A huge dining hall with a chandelier. Kayla was there and another woman. A witch called Eve. I've never seen her before." Tanner shudders and grips the seat with his fingernails. "She's powerful, and she's into F.H.B. in a *big* way. She drank from a human." He meets my eyes. "Guess who the human was?"

I shake my head.

"Johnny."

"Nova's ex?"

Tanner nods. "The guy I jumped into? His job was to take Johnny somewhere to be drained."

"So, they're selling F.H.B. as well as planning to overthrow the human race?" Mack asks.

Tanner takes a long swig of water and nods. "I didn't go with him for that part, but before I left, I saw something from the window." He takes his phone from his pocket, types something into Google Maps, then hands it to me and taps the screen. "I saw this."

I study the image. "The Red Rock railway station?"

"There's only one building opposite the railway station that's big enough to have six floors and a basement." Tanner takes his phone back and sinks into the seat. We have our answer. He can rest now.

I turn to Mack. His jaw twitches. "Looks like we're heading for The Red Tower."

"Looks like it." I take out my lighter and flick it open. For once, Mack doesn't object when I make the flame surge then put it out. "Are we ready?" I ask him. Glancing back at Tanner, I lower my voice. "Because it looks like this is going to be just the three of us versus a clan of wolves, an all-powerful witch, and who-the-fuck-knows what else they've got on their side."

Mack rubs his beard. A growl rumbles in this throat. "They took our girl and they hurt our brother." He slams his foot down on the accelerator. "The way I'm feeling right now? We'll rip them apart if we have to. But we *will* get our people out of there."

Behind us, there's movement. Tanner has opened his eyes. They look different. Darker yet brighter at the same time. "Fuck the witch, and fuck the wolves," he says. "I'm in the mood for a fight."

27

NOVA

We sleep until they come for us; pain and the release of our orgasms making us long for rest.

This time, they take us both together. The same wolves that marched Johnny center stage growl at me, one either side, and herd me into the elevator.

Behind us, Eve loops her chain back around Kole's neck and pulls him out of his cage. She sniffs the air, looks at both of us, and grins. "Seems like we're going to have to change our routine. Clearly, this morning's games got you two all *riled* up."

Instead of going to the roof, we're taken to a large room that looks like a lecture theater. Raised seating, filled with the same hungry hoard as earlier, curves around a wooden stage.

Eve pushes me onto it. Kayla sits in the front row, legs crossed, arms folded. She flashes Eve a look that says, *this better work*, and sucks in her cheeks.

Shoving Kole to one side, Eve claps to get everyone's attention. They were already staring at her but now they're quiet.

She doesn't speak to them, just turns to me and says, "Take a seat."

I blink at her.

She gestures to an empty seat next to Kayla and repeats herself. "I said, take a seat, Fire Bird."

I do as she says, my heart twisting in my chest as I leave Kole, bruised and weakened, with Eve. I look around, searching for someone holding a vial of F.H.B., but see no one.

Eve clicks her fingers and a young boy, who can't be more than fourteen or fifteen, runs onto the stage holding a wooden stool. She pushes Kole onto it and then looks into the wings. Another boy, slightly older, wheels out what looks like a metal coat stand.

Kole studies it. His eyes widen. *Nova. Don't be afraid.*

My throat constricts. Fear hammers my rib cage.

Eve lifts something and hooks it onto the top of the stand. It's a clear plastic pouch full of deep red liquid.

As I realize what she's doing, I have to force myself to stay seated. My muscles stiffen. My palms become hot. My eyes flash.

Kayla is watching me.

I start to tremble.

Stroking Kole's hair as if she's his mother or a nurse, Eve takes a needle, finds a vein, and pushes it into Kole's arm. Then she hooks up a long transparent tube. One end is connected to the needle, the other to the bag of what I now know is blood.

"In five minutes, this F.H.B. will hit Kole's veins," Eve says loudly, fixing her piercingly dark eyes on me. "It will continue to pump into him until the bag is empty."

Nausea settles like lead in my stomach.

"In the meantime, let's see if we can give you a little more motivation to reveal your true colors."

Kole's fists are clenched. He closes his eyes. I don't know what he's thinking, but I know I have to do something to stop this happening.

"We have another surprise for you, Nova." Eve waves her arms in the air excitedly. She's never used my name before. It makes me shiver. "We have a... special guest. Someone very close to your heart."

I almost jolt from my chair. Tanner? Is she talking about Tanner?

Kole looks like he's in a trance. His eyes are still closed. He's barely even breathing.

Eve jumps up and down. Her boots click on the wooden stage. "Ta *daaaah*." She holds out her arm.

There's a pause but then a figure stumbles out beside her as if he's been pushed. He steadies himself and straightens up.

My eyes widen. It can't be...

"Ladies and gentlemen, please welcome, the human sympathizer, the celebrity super, the werewolf who truly *cares*... Nico Varlac!" As Eve shouts her introduction like a voiceover artist on a commercial, the audience erupts into boos, hisses, and jeers.

Nico— the werewolf from TV— stares at them wide-eyed. He's dressed smartly in a shirt and slacks. His jet-black hair is slicked back, shiny but somehow still fluid. His jaw is chiseled, his eyes a deep hazel shade of brown. He smiles as if he's on a talk show, laughs nervously, and runs his fingers through his hair. "Listen, guys, whatever this is, we can talk about it. If you want money, I have money."

Eve laughs loudly. Kayla doesn't.

"Does anything about this man seem familiar to you, Fire Bird?" Eve pushes Nico a little closer to me. He stumbles and his smile drops. He still thinks he can charm his way free, doesn't he? I feel like yelling at him to run, to shift and break free.

Before I can, Eve strokes the side of Nico's face and says, "Does he remind you of anyone?"

With another nervous laugh, Nico says, "I'm sure she's seen me on TV." He meets my eyes and purposefully raises his eyebrows as if he wants me to answer the question so we can all go home. "Right? You've seen me on TV?"

"Yes, I've seen you," I speak slowly. There's something about his face. Something…

"Why don't you come on up and shake his hand?" Eve reaches for me, grabs my arm, and pulls me back on stage.

Nico does as he's told and extends his hand to shake mine.

I take it but when I look down at his fingers, my blood runs cold. I tilt his wrist. "You have a birthmark," I whisper.

Nico shrugs. "Yeah. Had it since… well, birth." He looks at Eve and tries to take his hand back. "Listen, whatever's going on here, I–"

She silences him with a *shhh* and studies my face.

"I've seen this before." I move my thumb to trace the deep purple mark on Nico's hand. Between his thumb and his wrist, shaped like a bird.

As realization hits me, I jolt backward.

Nico frowns and rubs his hand. "Fuck. She just gave me a static shock or something." He flexes his fingers. His palm is bright red. Singed by mine because I couldn't control the heat. "Look, this is clearly some kind of coven. Right? Whatever the game is. I'm out." Nico moves to stride off stage, but two snarling wolves stop him. He rolls his eyes. "I'm a werewolf too, you fuck-wits. I could–"

"Shut up!" In a momentary loss of cool, Eve yells at him. She lowers her voice, relaxes her tone, and smiles thinly. "Shut up and come say hi to your sister."

* * *

For a moment, everything goes quiet. I feel like I'm underwater, seeing shimmering, not-quite-there versions of the people around me. "Sam?" I whisper my brother's name. An image flashes through my mind. We're in our living room. Playing dinosaurs. Sam has a T-Rex. He's holding it, making it roar. On his hand is… the birthmark.

I stride forward and grab Nico's hand again. I'm losing control. Fire swirls inside me but all I can think about is that mark.

He's looking down at me. "Nova?" His eyes widen. He puts his hands on my upper arms and stares at me. He takes a strand of hair between his fingers and shakes his head. "My sister had auburn hair and she… she died." He shakes his head and moves away from me.

"What else do you remember about your sister?" Eve asks, standing between us, swaying from side to side.

Nico scrapes his fingers through his hair and breathes out hard. "She was older than me. Just a year. Her parents fostered me when I was five. She was six. We used to fight a lot." He chuckles at the memory. He's still studying my face. "I didn't know I was a werewolf. One day, I…" He clears his throat. "I bit her when we were playing, and I don't know how she did it, but she started a… a fire."

I'm trembling from head to toe. I look at Kole. He's opened his eyes. He's staring at us. Blood is creeping toward the needle in his arm, snaking down the clear plastic tube. *Nova, it's okay. Don't give in.*

"They told me she died. Sent me to a foster home for supers. I was adopted." Nico's speaking to me now, as if he knows I need to hear this.

"They told me the same." I can't stop looking at the birthmark. "They told me my brother died."

Nico looks from me to Eve. "I don't understand," he breathes.

"It can't be you." I shake my head and move backward away from him. My skin fizzes.

"Smoke! She's smoking!" someone yells.

I don't care. In this moment, I don't care. Memories pummel my brain. The ones Kole showed me. More. The hospital. Doctors leaning over my bed. *We're so sorry, your brother is gone. Your parents too.* My first foster home. My second. My third.

I grip my head and shake it.

"Nova!" Kole shouts to me and tries to stand but Eve ticks her head sideways and he crashes back onto the stool.

"You can't be my brother. My brother died." I shake my arms, try to hold back the tsunami of emotion that's barreling through me.

Nico puts his hand on my arm. "Nova?" he asks, meeting my eyes. "Nova? Is it you?"

"You can't be him. It's a lie." Sparks fly into the air. The ground beneath my feet grows hot. I look down. The floor is glowing.

"Here..." Nico reaches for his shirt. "Look..." He unfastens the top three buttons and pulls it open, then the next, then the next.

I press my palm to his chest. It's mottled with burns. Raised, twisted skin covers his torso.

"Nova!" Kole calls to me but the sound seems distant.

I run my hand over Nico's chest.

"My name hasn't always been Nico," he says, taking hold of my hand and pressing it to his chest. I feel his heart beating beneath my fingers. "Before the fire, I was called Sam."

My brother's name reverberates in my head. *Sam.* I blink at him through watery eyes.

"They took me. Did they take you?" Nico grips my hand tighter.

"Nova, stop!" Kole roars at me. I look at him. The blood has almost reached him. One more minute and it'll be inside him.

It's too much. It's all too much. I step back, shaking. I stretch out my arms, spin around and send a blast of fire toward the IV. It severs the tube. I send another that knocks the metal stand flying. Blood sloshes free, soaking the floor.

Kole's eyes roll in his head as the scent of iron fills the air.

Eve is watching me with glee. She stands back. Kayla remains seated.

I scream. I reach up toward the ceiling and send a wave of flame from my palms. It hits the roof and takes hold. Flames crawl down the walls and start licking the floor. The crowd begins to panic. They stand and scrabble toward the back of the room.

An alarm sounds. Water rains down from the ceiling but it doesn't put out my fire. I send more, snaking through the aisles.

As the doors swing open and members of the League spill out into the corridor, some shifting, some running in human form, I storm after them. I want to burn them. All of them.

I'm at the door when something grips hold of me. I strain against it, but it pulls me back. I fight it but it's no use. I'm flung onto the ground. Hands grab my arms and drag me back to the stage.

Someone opens my mouth and pours a hot acidic liquid into it. Then they slam it shut and pinch my nose until I swallow, spluttering and choking.

My eyes feel heavy. I turn my head. Kole is surrounded by flames, but I can't reach him.

28

MACK

The building is on fire. Alarms wail. Smoke billows from the windows.

"There." Tanner points. "Third floor. The smoke is worse there."

I nod, already beginning to shift.

As my muscles stretch and grow, a familiar ripping sensation tears through me. It never gets easier, but it does get quicker.

Let's find our girl, I mutter to Snow. He growls in agreement.

Running ahead of the others, we head straight for the side of the building, Tanner and Luther close behind us. It used to be a hotel. According to Google, it was taken over a few years ago for luxury apartments. Clearly, that was a ruse.

Round back, as expected, we find the old laundry entrance. We barrel into it without hesitating. The doors quake beneath Snow's mammoth shoulders.

We sniff the air. Blood, water, smoke.

The others follow us. Through more doors, down a long corridor, to a stairwell. We head up, the scent of blood getting stronger. We're almost at the top when sprinklers start pounding water onto the steps.

The building vibrates with alarms; fire alarms and security alarms.

We emerge in another hallway. This one has a shiny marble floor and doors lining its sides. We're at the end of it with Luther on one side and Tanner on the other, when we run into a pack of fucking wolves.

Snow and I stop, rise up onto our hind legs, and release a growl that makes our chest swell and our muscles tremble.

Luther and Tanner stand stock still. The wolves whimper and turn tail. They run right. So, we go left.

The smoke is thicker here. *Small breaths, buddy,* I tell Snow. *Small breaths.* Because our lungs already feel tight.

Tanner takes the blindfold from his pocket and uses it to cover his mouth, Luther uses his shirt. But when we reach the doors, they drop their shields. Something *powerful* is in that room; they need their hands. They need their magick.

Luther pushes the door. Whatever is inside is obscured by smoke and water. It rains down in thick sheets from the ceiling. Tanner flicks his hands out to his sides. He's drenched, water running off his face and soaking his clothes. His eyes shimmer. He waves his hands, and the water parts.

Now it's Luther's turn. He blows a plume of clean air from his mouth. It grows, and grows, and pushes the smoke away. Flames still lap at the walls but there are too many for him to put out alone.

Five figures are on a large wooden stage. Snow's heart beats faster. A rumble escapes his lips as we charge toward it.

One of the figures, a witch, spins around and attempts to knock us flying. Her magick is strong, but not strong enough to toss an eight-hundred-kilo bear. Snow and I head straight for her. The other woman shifts into a wolf and dives from the stage.

Luther throws a fire ball at her. It catches her tail, and she yelps. Tanner brings a torrent of water down from the ceiling, knocks her from her paws, and sends her sliding back down the aisle toward us.

Snow and I tackle the witch. She's backing away.

Tanner yells, "Luther, take Nova!" He tries to grab the wolf, but she finds her footing and sprints from the room.

Our eyes rove the stage. There she is. Our supernova. She's on the ground. She looks groggy. Someone is bent over her but it's not Kole. It's a werewolf. We can smell him.

Luther takes him by the neck and throws him off her, but she grabs Luther's arms and yells, "No! Luther! Nico's my brother!"

Brother? Nico? The fucking werewolf from the talk shows?

I turn back to the witch. She's standing behind Kole. He's on a stool, head lolling onto his chest, but still sitting upright. She grabs a fistful of his hair and jerks his head back.

Tanner yells again, "Luther! Get Nova *out of here!*"

The witch is holding a knife. She brings it to Kole's throat. "Let me go," she says, "or I gut him right now."

We stop, breathing heavily.

Tanner holds out his hand. "Snow, wait."

The witch studies us for a moment then drops the knife and runs. As she disappears, Kole falls to the floor.

Snow and I stoop down, and Tanner heaves Kole onto our back.

"Luther, fucking go!" Tanner yells. "Take the car. We'll meet you at The Hollow. Get Nova *home*."

"I'm not leaving without Nico." Nova meets Tanner's eyes. He nods at her. "I'll make sure he gets out. Now, go!"

29

NOVA

Luther has hold of my hand. We race down a corridor and around a corner. Sprinklers rain water, slicking the marble floor beneath our feet and drenching our clothes. He looks back at me over his shoulder. "Nearly there."

We turn another corner at the exact moment a wolf skids around the one up ahead. We meet, staring at each other. The wolf bares its teeth. It snarls. I can't identify who it is, and I don't care.

At the same time, Luther and I pull fire into our palms and throw two huge balls hurtling in the wolf's direction. They're dampened by the sprinklers but not extinguished. The wolf leaps to the side but skids and thuds into the wall. While it's righting itself, Luther pulls me through a door to our left.

We're in a stairwell. The lights flicker. He tugs me down and I follow him.

We've taken three flights when we finally reach the bottom. There's a fire exit in front of us. "It leads to the street. I saw it on the way in..." Luther trails off. Something makes him turn back toward the stairs. I heard it too.

I step sideways, peering into the dark crevice beneath the steps. Someone's there. Someone's crying.

I move forward two paces, but Luther grabs my arm.

"Come out," he says, conjuring blue fire this time that casts the room in an eerie glow.

The figure unfolds itself and stands up, using the wall for support. When they step into the light, my chest lurches with disgust.

"Johnny," I breathe.

He looks at me with watery eyes. He's wearing a torn vest. The skin that's exposed is raw and covered in burns. Burns *I* gave him. There's a wound on his neck and another on the inside of his arm. He is so pale he's almost not there at all.

He staggers forward. His hair is slick with grease. He reaches for me and, instinctively, I catch him. With his fingers on my arm, he meets my eyes. Luther is watching us. I wait. I expect him to grovel like he did when we were surrounded by flames and he was afraid of me.

Instead, he rolls his tongue around his mouth, juts his head back, and spits in my face.

As I wipe the moisture from my eyes, my skin crawling, Luther grabs Johnny by the throat and yells, "You son of a bitch." Holding him there, he says to me, "Let me bring him. Me and the guys will teach this pathetic bastard what happens to men who beat their women."

But something has settled inside me. Not fear or humiliation—the two feelings I've associated with Johnny for longer than I can count. Something else; a deep and powerful knowledge that he hates me because he sees something in me. A fire he wants to dampen. A spirit he has tried his best to put out.

I tug at Luther's arm. "Let him go. I'll teach him myself."

Luther hesitates but when my hand grows hot on his skin, he backs up.

Johnny wipes his mouth with the back of his hand. He's barely able to stand up but he still thinks he's more powerful than me. He opens his mouth to speak but before a sound can come out, I step back, close my eyes, stretch out my arms, and roar.

It's an ear-splitting roar. It rises above the noise of the fire alarms and the sprinklers. Above the sirens outside. It comes from a place so deep inside me that my entire body starts to shake. I snap my head back and open my palms at Johnny. I don't want fire this time, I want heat.

I stare at him. I see the time he branded me with the poker. I see the time he smashed my head against the kitchen worktop. I see the scars, the blood, the nights he forced me to fuck him and made me pretend to enjoy it. I see the way I was when I met him—young and desperate to be taken care of—and the way I was when I left Ridgemore—a shadow of the person I once was.

I channel it, all of it, every morsel of shame and degradation and anger. And I use it to set fire to him from the inside out.

He clutches his stomach. He doubles over and drops to his knees. Next, he reaches for his throat. His face is red, he can't breathe.

Blood trickles from his nose, his eyes, his ears. He coughs. More blood, on his vest and the floor and on me.

He starts to smoke. His skin looks like lava, like it's turning to liquid and splitting open.

There's a sickly crackle and a pop, and then he explodes.

And pieces of Johnny decorate the walls.

* * *

I STAND FOR A LONG MOMENT, unable to move. Then Luther grabs me and pulls me to the door. "We have to go, now." He takes my hand and drags me outside. We run across the parking lot at the back of the building to a wire fence. Beyond it there are trees. I can see the guys' car in the distance.

I start to shake. I lift a strand of my hair and look at it; it's drenched with blood. I pick something out of it. Something fleshy and soft.

Nausea jolts into my throat. I vomit onto the floor in front of me. When I look up, Luther puts his hands on my upper arms.

"It's okay."

"I killed him," I whisper, eyes wide.

"It's okay," Luther repeats.

"But... I killed him."

"He deserved it." Luther meets my eyes and nods solemnly. "He deserved it, Nova. He's gone now. He can't hurt you or anyone else."

"But he was unarmed. He couldn't hurt me... and I killed him anyway."

"I know what you're feeling." He pulls me to his chest, seeming not to care that pieces of Johnny are splattered all over me. He squeezes me tight. He's warm. His heat spreads to my chest. "It will be okay, but right now..." He steps back and takes my hand. "We have to get out of here."

Above us, every window in the building is alight. The top blazes so bright it illuminates the sky. Sirens indicate that police and firefighters are on their way. A wolf howls. Then another. The sound sends a chill down my spine.

Luther nods at me and we run.

30

LUTHER

In the car, Nova turns to me, chest shaking as she breathes heavily in and out. "The others... we can't leave them, not after everything." She moves to open the car door, but I press the locks down and shake my head.

"After everything, the most important thing is keeping you safe." As I reverse, the wheels screech. There's an electronic barrier blocking the way to the road, but I rev the engine and hurtle toward it at top speed. It flies into the air, bounces off the hood, and smashes into pieces as it hits the tarmac.

I don't look at Nova until we're through the tunnel and back on the winding road toward Phoenix Falls. When I do, she's still shaking, drenched, freezing cold, covered in remnants of her ex-boyfriend.

I told her I knew what she was going through because I do; I've killed for revenge. But I've never done that—burned someone from the inside out. I wouldn't even know how.

She's looking at her hands as if she can't quite believe it either.

"Setting fire to the roof—that was deliberate. I wanted to do it. I knew how." She's speaking softly, almost as if she's talking to herself. "But Johnny..." She swallows hard and turns to look out of the window. "I didn't plan it but as soon as it started happening, I knew I didn't want to stop. I *wanted* him dead."

I put my hand on her thigh then take it back—it should be Tanner comforting her, or Kole, heck even Mack, not me.

"Nico?" I ask her, partly to change the subject and partly because I need to know what's going on with the guy she insisted on saving. "The werewolf from the TV? The one who does all the speeches? You said he was your brother, but I thought your brother was called Sam."

Nova looks out at the stars and sighs a heavy sigh. "Nico *is* Sam."

I frown. "Nova, how's that possible?"

"He survived the fire, but they never told me. He was sent to a different care home. He found a nice family. Grew up with nice parents. Went to college..."

"And the rest is history," I mutter. "Does he have proof?"

She nods. She's crying now, tears merging with blood and streaming down her face. She doesn't wipe them away. "Sam had a birthmark on his hand." She rubs the spot between her thumb and her wrist. "Nico has the same birthmark. And he has..." She bites her lower lip. "Scars. From the fire." She looks at me and nods. "It's him, Luther. Why else would the League risk kidnapping a celebrity, if not to torture me?"

As she turns back to the window and sinks into pained silence, I grip the wheel and concentrate on the road. Nico might tick all the right boxes to make Nova believe he's her long-lost brother, but I'm not going to take anything the League says as fact.

And I'm pretty sure the other guys won't either.

* * *

When we pull up to The Hollow, it's in darkness. The protection spells seem to be holding because we've yet to be vandalized like Rev's.

I open the car door for Nova and help her out.

"The others aren't back yet?" she asks, searching the house for signs of movement within.

"Doesn't look like it. Let's go inside and get you cleaned up."

As she walks beside me, she stumbles. I put my arm around her waist. At the top of the steps, I look down at her. She's shorter than me and softer. She has curved edges and big eyes. Right now, in this moment, the vehement dislike I felt for her when she arrived in town seems to have vanished. Right now, all I see is someone who is incredibly brave. Someone who has already had to survive too much in her relatively short life.

"Nova," I say, arm still around her. "I'm glad you're safe."

She looks at me, and something that's almost a smile curls her lips. "You don't even like me, Luther."

I clear my throat. "Maybe not, but I like staying alive and rumor has it you're the key to that happening."

Her eyes search my face. She nudges into me and nods. A laugh tickles her throat. "Thanks, Luther." For a moment, she rests her head on my shoulder. The sound of an engine in the distance makes her stand up straight.

I step in front of her, hands ready to throw fire if they need to. But then I see a flash of white, and a truck rolls into the drive. The flash of white? Snow. A huge fucking polar bear riding in the back of a truck that doesn't belong to any one of us.

When the truck stops, Tanner jumps out and runs to

release the tailgate. Snow moves aside and climbs down as Tanner swaps places with him.

Nova darts past me and runs down the steps. When she reaches the truck, she gasps and reaches for Tanner's hand so he can pull her up beside him. "Kole?" She turns to Tanner. "He's unconscious?"

"He'll be okay. Let's get him inside." Tanner looks past Nova toward me. "Luther, help me get him onto Snow's back."

I take the steps two at a time. Kole looks like hell. Snow positions himself at the end of the truck and dips his head while Tanner and I pull Kole's Viking-sized frame toward him.

Somehow, we heave Kole onto Snow and loop his arms around the bear's neck. Kole groans. His eyes flutter open.

"Hold on to Snow," Tanner says, reaching up to help Kole weave his fingers into Snow's fur.

Kole slumps forward onto Snow's neck but manages to hold on as the bear carries him to the house.

Helping Nova down from the truck, Tanner notices her clothes. "Nova, what happened?" He runs his hands down her arms, cups her face in his hands, and presses his forehead to hers.

"I'm alright." She places her hands on top of his. I feel as if I should look away. "I'm alright." She kisses him, softly at first and then with the hunger you'd expect from someone who has recently almost died. Tanner pulls her to his chest.

"You found me." She hugs him tight. "You found me. I knew you would. Kole said you would. I'm so sorry I left like that. I didn't know what to do. I'm sorry I kept it from you."

When Tanner pulls back and smiles at her, she smiles back. "You have nothing to apologize for," he says, stroking her blood-stained cheek.

I look away. Whatever is passing unsaid between them is too intimate for me to see. My gaze lands on the truck. Leaning on the passenger side door, Nico the werewolf is watching Nova too.

When he catches me noticing him, his expression changes. A moment ago, he was intrigued. Now, he looks suddenly exhausted. A little traumatized. Weak. The change was too fast… something about it makes my stomach clench.

I follow him closely as he walks behind Nova and Tanner up the steps to The Hollow's front door.

He scratches at something on the back of his neck. I move closer. There's a shadow beneath the collar of his shirt. A shadow I can't quite make out. A tattoo? A birthmark?

Inside, as Nova and Tanner run to the lounge to tend to Kole, Snow shifts back into Mack.

Nico doesn't flinch, looks approvingly at Mack's naked form, and holds out a hand to shake his.

Mack hesitates but takes it.

"Thank you," Nico says, looking from Mack to me. "I don't know who the heck you guys are but thank you. You saved my life, and my sister's."

Mack takes his hand back and stalks to the cupboard near the door. He pulls sweatpants and a white tee from inside it and hurriedly steps into them.

"Can I see her?" Nico asks, moving toward the lounge.

"No," Mack's answer is firm. "Leave her."

Nico looks as if he's about to object, but I cut him off. "Tanner's a nurse. He'll fix her up." In my most polite voice, I add, "You must be pretty shaken. Come, we'll get you a drink."

"Something a little stronger than tea, I hope?" Nico asks in a far too relaxed voice.

"Whatever you need, buddy." I pat his back. "Any friend of Nova's is a friend of ours."

But as we lead him to the kitchen, Mack and I exchange a look we've exchanged many times before—something about this guy doesn't sit right.

This guy is *not* to be trusted. Even if he is Nico-fucking-Varlac.

31

NOVA

The fire in the lounge is lit. As Tanner fetches his medical bag from the window seat, he looks at Kole, who's lying on the couch, then at me as if he's totally torn. He runs his hands over me, checking for injuries, and looks at the bite wound on my chest. I shake my head and tell him, "I'm okay. Kole took the worst of it. Help him first."

Squeezing my hand, Tanner kneels and strokes Kole's hair back from his face and Kole's eyes slowly open. I sit next to Kole's legs and rest my hand on his thigh. Thick like a tree trunk, sturdy, but wounded.

"It's okay. We've got you." Tanner smiles as Kole groans and tries to sit up.

"We're back home," I tell him. "We're okay." I put my other hand on Tanner's back. His muscles twitch at the pressure.

There's a knock on the door as Mack enters. He's holding a stack of towels and a jug of water. "Thought you might need these," he says quietly, setting them down nearby.

I stand up and take his elbow, pulling him into the corner of the room. "Nico? He's okay?"

Mack cups my face with his hand. He nods. His eyes bore into mine. "He's okay."

"I should…" I look back at Tanner and Kole. I can't leave them, but my *brother* is in this house.

"You should take care of Kole, and yourself. Nico can wait until morning." Mack brings my gaze back to his and fixes me with a look that makes me wonder whether Luther has already told him what I did. "You need to rest. There'll be time to digest what happened. But not yet." He closes the door as he leaves.

On the couch, Kole winces as Tanner touches the bruise on his side. "Couple of broken ribs," he says.

"Only a couple?" Kole replies through gritted teeth.

Tanner has lifted something from his bag. Some kind of liquid in a small blue bottle. He supports Kole's head and tells him to drink.

"What is it?" I ask, setting the towels down on the coffee table.

"It'll help the pain." Tanner squeezes Kole's shoulder.

Kole screws up his eyes and rolls his tongue around his mouth.

"Fucking revolting," he spits, but almost instantly he seems a little brighter.

"It's not a miracle cure but it'll take the edge off. I haven't mastered setting bones yet, so not sure you want me to…"

"Do it." Kole cuts him off. "I trust you."

Tanner breathes in, flexes his fingers, then closes his eyes and presses his hands to Kole's chest. He starts to whisper.

Bae sra vuvar uk sra ksork, raor srek braod.

Bae sra vuvar uk sra kuum, koda bumak vrura.

The words are foreign and utterly beautiful on his tongue. I breathe them in and, as Tanner repeats them, I find they're no longer strange but familiar. I understand them.

By the power of the stars, heal these breaks.

By the power of the moon, make these bones whole.

My eyes widen. At the same time, Kole cries out, there's a cracking sound, he grasps his ribs, but then his muscles untense.

"It worked." He smiles at Tanner. "You did it."

Tanner sits back on his heels. He's pale. Kole has noticed too.

"What else did you do for us today?"

Tanner shakes his head and looks away, but Kole brings his hand to Tanner's jaw and brings his gaze back to him.

"Tanner… how did you find us?"

A shudder runs down Tanner's back. He visibly shakes. "Later," he says, touching Kole's fingers while he turns to look at me. "I'll tell you both later."

Standing up, he says to Kole, "You'll feel rough for a while. You need to rest."

"I also need…" Kole pushes himself up so he's resting on the cushions. "The witch, she gave me something. It dulled my powers. I used what little I had left back in the warehouse, since then I've been next to useless."

"She gave it to me too. After I…" Shame flushes my cheeks as I remember how I lost control. I move to the couch and slot my fingers between Kole's. "I'm so sorry. I couldn't stop it…"

"You did good." Kole tucks a strand of hair behind my ear. "You did really good, Little Star." Then he frowns at me. "Is that blood?" His nose wrinkles.

I stand up and pace away from him. Tanner follows me. "Nova? Let me see." He tries to look at my head, assuming the blood is mine, but I duck away.

"It's not mine." I screw my eyes shut as the sound of Johnny's body splattering the walls, and my hair, and my face, rings in my ears. When I open my eyes, Kole and Tanner are staring at me. "It's Johnny's."

"Johnny's?" Kole tries to turn so he's angled toward me, but the movement makes him groan and stop.

"When Luther and I escaped, we found him in the stairwell. He…" I shake my arms as prickly heat snakes down them. "I thought he wanted help, but he spat in my face."

Tanner's eyes flash with fury but then soften. A smile twitches his lips. He exchanges a knowing glance with Kole. "So, Luther finished him?"

I inhale slowly then shake my head. "Not Luther… me."

"You?" Tanner frowns.

I sit down hard on the window seat, and by the time I've finished telling them what happened, I'm sobbing.

Tanner kneels in front of me and pulls me onto his lap, cradling me like a child. Kole pushes himself up from the couch and limps over. He lowers himself to the floor and runs his hands up my back, rubbing me gently. "Shhh," Tanner whispers, "it's okay. It'll be okay."

Still holding me tight, Tanner looks at Kole. "She needs to wash this asshole off her."

Kole nods and levers himself up using the window seat. He heads for the old-fashioned writing desk in the corner of the room and reaches beneath it. There's a clicking sound then something whirrs. I look up from Tanner's chest to see the space around the coffee table jolt down, just an inch. A line has appeared in a rectangle around it. The table starts to sink. A hole appears. A huge, dark hole. Then the floor rises back up. Except, this time, there's a white bathtub where the coffee table once was. It has high, curved walls but no taps.

Tanner helps me up and passes me to Kole. He wraps his arms around me and holds me while Tanner fetches the jug Mack brought us and the towels.

He places the towels on the couch then offers me his hand. He helps me climb in. Kole follows me and sits on the edge.

Without speaking, Tanner peels off my top and unhooks my bra. Kole removes my jeans, steadying me as he tugs them over my feet. When he hooks his thumbs in my panties, he looks up at me.

A smile flutters across my lips.

Instead of taking them off gently, Kole pulls them hard. The seam rips and he holds them up.

Tanner frowns.

"I'll explain later," Kole says, tossing the underwear to the floor.

Now I'm exposed, I look down at myself. Johnny's blood has seeped through my clothes and onto my skin. He is in my hair, on my face, under my nails.

Tears bite at my throat but, as if he knows, Tanner presses his thumb to the exact spot where the emotion sits and strokes it.

Kole stands up and steadies me, one hand on my waist, the other tracing the lines and swirls of ink he adorned on my chest. Tanner lifts the jug. When he tilts it, a never-ending stream of warm water pours from the spout. He starts with my hair, eases my head back and washes it clean. Then the two of them turn their attention to my body.

Together, they use their hands to scrub Johnny's remnants from my skin. They smooth their beautiful large palms over every inch of me. Tanner gently washes the bite wound on my collarbone then kisses it. The jug is now suspended, levitating above me, and the water keeps coming.

Tanner reaches my hips at the same moment Kole reaches my breasts. As Kole sweeps his thumbs beneath them and his fingers graze my nipples, Tanner smooths warm water between my legs.

A small moan passes my lips. I reach for Kole. He kisses me, his tongue caressing mine. Arousal throbs in my core.

Tanner sits me down in the tub. This time, when he pours

water in a cascade down my back, it doesn't drain away. It stays and fills the tub. Tanner takes something from his bag and puts a few drops into the water. A soft foam forms on its surface.

The tub is large. Large enough for three.

"Join me," I say, tugging Kole and Tanner's belts at the same time.

Tanner turns to Kole. Without speaking, he unfastens Kole's pants and rolls them over his hips. His dick is already hard. It pops free. Tanner swipes his thumb over a bead of pre-cum on its tip.

I lean back in the bath, letting the warm water into all the places I want to welcome Tanner and Kole.

Kole's breath is heavy, his muscles ripple as his chest rises and falls. Tanner moves closer to him and dips his head to lap at the bruise on Kole's ribs.

Winding his fingers into Tanner's hair, Kole groans then tugs Tanner's shirt over his head. When it's on the floor, he makes him stand up straight and turns him around. "Show our girl what you've got for her," he growls.

Dutifully, Tanner removes his jeans and his boxers. His dick is perfect. He moves toward me, but Kole reaches around from behind and cups his balls.

Tanner stops, releases a loud moan, and tips his head back as Kole's fingers settle around his throat. He squeezes, just a little, and Tanner lets out a stifled breath.

"Bring him here for me." I don't sit up. My clit is desperate to be touched, but I don't want to be the one to do it.

Kole nudges Tanner forward, his cock pressing against Tanner's tight bare ass.

I lift a sopping wet hand and curl my fingers around Tanner's shaft. While Kole tugs his balls, I lower my mouth and trail a row of kisses from his base to his tip. When I reach his shining slit, I swirl my tongue over it. Tanner's legs weaken. Kole releases his throat. He breathes out heavily.

"Get in the tub. Sit behind her." Kole stands back and watches as I make room for Tanner.

"You too?" I ask, desperate to pull him toward me.

Kole shakes his head. A wry smile parts his lips as he looks down at his injured body. "Not sure I'm up to it yet, Little Star. But if you're a good girl, and do as I say, I'll make it up to you as soon as I'm able."

The words *good girl* make me sink lower in the water and pull Tanner's fingers to my clit. He toys with it while his other hand rolls my nipples between his fingers. As he presses down on my pussy, he pinches my nipple. I lean into his chest and reach up to loop my hands behind his head. He kisses my neck. His teeth graze my skin, and his dick grows rock hard beneath my ass.

"Do you want to?" I ask, knowing how close we came when we were in the lake. Knowing how badly I want to experience a *first time* with Tanner so I can erase the night I lost my virginity to Johnny in the back of his truck.

Tanner moans into my neck but then looks up at Kole. "Not yet. Not until Kole can fuck you at the same time."

I turn to look at Kole too. He's not touching himself, just watching us, hands behind his back. I beckon him closer then, while Tanner slides a finger into my cunt, I take Kole in my mouth. He lets me lick and suck then starts to thrust. I tilt my head, so his tip hits the inside of my cheek. He releases a long, low, "Ahhhh," at the pressure.

Then he moves sideways, takes his dick away from me, and pulls Tanner's mouth toward him instead. He gives Tanner three hard thrusts then returns to me.

Tanner and I press our cheeks together and leave our mouths open so Kole can move quickly between us, dipping in and out. He holds the backs of our heads. Then he takes my hands and pulls me up so I'm kneeling, my upper half bent over the bathtub.

Tanner stands, braces one leg on the tub, finds my pussy, and eases into me. As he grinds his hips into me, my tits hit the cold porcelain of the bathtub, and his balls slap my pussy.

I reach for Kole and bring his dick to my mouth. At first, our rhythm is out of sync but then Kole locks his gaze on Tanner's, and they fuck me in tandem. As Tanner thrusts into me from behind, Kole leans back. When Kole inches his dick further into my mouth, Tanner's hips sway backward.

Tanner reaches down and swirls his finger around my clit. I hold on to the tub. Kole strokes my hair from my face. He kisses my forehead. The gesture is tender and surprising and makes me whine with pleasure. Tanner has found the perfect rhythm for my clit. His arm muscles are tense with the effort of not breaking the pattern of circles and pressure. My body stiffens. I cry out but it's swallowed by Kole's cock. He's going to come. I can feel him getting harder and bigger. He lifts my face so I'm looking up at him, and I almost choke as his cum fills my mouth.

He pulls out. Cum dribbles down my chin, but I swallow the rest. I push my ass back against Tanner then turn and make him sit down.

Straddling him in the water, I slide onto his cock and start to move up and down, grinding to my own rhythm, pressing my clit into him.

He looks at my mouth and cups my face. Bringing my lips to his, he licks them slowly then cleans Kole's cum from my chin with his tongue. He jerks up into me.

Water splashes over the sides of the tub. I brace my hands on the back of it and slam my cunt down onto him, as if the force of it can push the pain and anguish of the past two days from my body.

"Oh, my stars, don't stop, Nova. Don't stop." Tanner wraps his arms around me. He's squeezing me hard.

"I'm going to come." I lean back so I can see his face. He palms my breasts, and his eyes widen. "Come with me!"

"Ladies…" Tanner winces as he tries to hold back. "First…"

An orgasm rolls through me. My walls flutter and grip his length, squeezing him until he comes. His cum fills me up but this time there's no fire. No heat.

I droop forward into his arms. He kisses me. I turn, knowing Kole will be there. He leans down and kisses my neck.

"I love you," I whisper. "Both of you."

Tanner plants a kiss on my injured collarbone. Kole strokes my wet hair. "I really need to sit down," he says, staggering back to the couch, laughing.

As Tanner helps me out of the tub and wraps me in a towel, he kisses me again. "No fireworks this time?"

I frown. "Oh, there were fireworks, just not the literal kind." I move to the couch and Kole pulls me onto his naked lap.

"Whatever Eve gave us is strong stuff." He flicks my hair from my shoulder. "But Tanner will fix us. He'll find a solution."

Tanner nods and kisses my forehead. "I'll call the hospital first thing."

"In the meantime," I look from one guy to the other and laugh at myself. "I'm starving. We didn't eat for two days. Can we…"

Tanner jumps to his feet. "You two stay there. Don't move. I'll bring snacks."

He's at the door when Kole says, "Tanner?"

"Mmm?" Tanner turns to look at us.

"Fuck the snacks. I need a burger."

"And fries," I add.

"And a milkshake…" Kole swings his legs around so he's stretched out on the couch cushions, and I'm nestled between his knees.

"And coffee." I lean back and close my eyes, yawning. "Definitely coffee."

I'm asleep before Tanner's left the room.

32

NOVA

The Hollow is silent when I wake. We are still downstairs, couch cushions spread out like a makeshift bed on the floor. Kole is behind me—the big spoon. Tanner is in front—the little spoon.

The remnants of our bath and our burgers—dutifully cooked by Tanner at well past midnight—litter the room. The fire has faded to just a delicate crackle in the grate.

Kole's arm is slung across my waist, his hand resting on Tanner's hip. As he stirs, so does his cock, but he doesn't open his eyes.

Slipping out of my mage sandwich, I pick up a throw from a nearby armchair and walk to the window. The sun is only just rising. We can't have had more than a few hours' sleep, yet I know I won't be able to close my eyes again.

I needed last night. *We* needed it. But now I have bigger things to do… I have to speak to my brother, and then to Mack because I cannot ever lose control again the way I did with Johnny. He needs to teach me how to harness my power, and he needs to teach me quickly. Because I'm certain this is only the beginning of our fight.

I pad past the guys, leaving them to sleep, and head up to my room. The few clothes I have left are in the dresser. I choose a fresh sweater, but I have no spare jeans. Stupid, to only have bought one pair.

I head for the bathroom in just my underwear and my sweater. I clean my teeth, splash cold water on my face, and brush my long ashen hair.

I'm walking past Mack's room to go find some of Tanner's sweatpants when Mack's door opens. "Nova?" He's butt naked. It's the second time I've seen his penis, but this time it's erect. He blinks sleepily at me and rubs his gray beard. "Nova?" He seems totally unfazed by the fact he's naked but when he realizes I'm staring, he darts behind the door and I hear him pulling on some boxers. "Are you alright?" He steps back into view, now reaching for a hoodie.

He tugs it over his head then notices that my legs are bare.

"My only pair of jeans is ruined. I was just..."

"Wait." Mack holds his hand up and grabs a pair of slacks. When he's fastened them, he ushers me inside. His room is meticulously neat, and very unlike what I expected. The rest of the house is old fashioned, but this room has gray walls, white sheets, and minimal decoration except for a plant on the windowsill and a large armchair.

"This isn't what I thought your bedroom would look like."

"You've thought about my bedroom?" Mack asks, smiling at me with a twinkle in his eye. The same twinkle he had when we first met in The Cross.

I shrug off the question. "Owning somewhere like The Hollow, I figured you liked *old* stuff."

Mack chuckles. "Ask me another time why I bought this place, but not right now." He walks to the end of his large bed. The only un-modern piece of furniture in the room is a wooden chest, butted up against the foot of the bed.

Mack opens it and stoops to move things around.

He pulls out a small bundle of clothes.

"Try these."

I frown at them. "Ex-girlfriend?" I ask, setting the pile down to examine it.

"No," Mack says, clearing his throat. "My sister."

I stand up, aware my ass is on display in my too-flimsy underwear. "I didn't know you had a sister." I smile a little. "I can't imagine a female Baloo. Is she devastatingly good looking?"

Mack hums at the use of his nickname, but a different kind of smile curves his lips. A sad smile. "She died when she was just a little younger than you are." He looks away from me and puts his hands into his pockets. "If it's too strange, you don't have to wear them. I just thought…" He looks out of the window at the brightening sky. "It's not safe for us to leave The Hollow right now, so…"

My chest twitches. I cross the room and take Mack's elbow. "Thank you," I say as he turns to meet my eyes. "The clothes are great."

I'm about to ask him his sister's name when the sound of footsteps thundering up the stairs makes us both jump.

"Nova?" Tanner's worried voice fills the hall. "Nova?" He reaches Mack's open door and flies in, sees me half-undressed, and stops. Hands on his hips, he looks us both up and down. He smiles. "Here I was panicking you'd left again, and I find you pants-down with the professor?" He laughs and flops down on the bed. It seems as if everyone needs a bit of light relief after yesterday, and I'm only too happy to oblige.

"What can I say?" I narrow my eyes and sashay my hips as I walk past him. "Last night wasn't *quite* satisfying enough for me."

I scoop up the clothes from the bed. Tanner tries to grab

me, but I duck free and run from the room laughing. He chases me down the hall back to our room, catches me, and tosses me onto the bed.

Climbing on top of me, he murmurs, "Last night wasn't *satisfying* enough for you?" He pins my arms above my head. "You want the professor to join in? Would that help?"

I giggle and pretend to try to break free from him. "Maybe."

Tanner kisses me. I bite his lower lip playfully and he sits back, adjusting the bulge in his boxers. His eyes sparkle, but I wriggle out from under him and pick up the pants Mack gave me. Black, a little tight, but better than oversized boyfriend pants.

Tanner releases a low whistle. "Shit, Little Star. Those pants make your ass look incredible."

He cups my ass cheeks and squeezes, but I bat away his hands. "You can compliment me later." A small shiver runs through me. "Right now, I need to go find my brother."

33

NOVA

Nico is already waiting in the kitchen. He looks like he slept here; creases on his cheek showing the spot where he rested his head in his arms. I stare at him for a moment, unable to make sense of who I'm looking at.

For years, when *Nico Varlac* appeared on TV, I was intrigued, drawn to him, like every other non-super-hating woman in the country. I thought it was because of his charm and his ridiculously square jaw. But maybe the whole time, it was something else.

He rubs a hand over his face and notices me. As he meets my eyes, the image of him on that late-night TV show flashes through my head. I see Johnny. I see Johnny's flesh in my hair. His blood on my skin. But then I remember Kole and Tanner's hands on my body, washing Johnny away. And the queasiness in my stomach fades.

Mack appears from the hall and starts making coffee. Tanner has followed me and is studying Nico closely.

"Morning." Nico stands up and extends his hand to shake Tanner's.

"Morning." Tanner takes it but doesn't look pleased.

"I'm sorry, this is odd. And an intrusion." Nico's cheeks flush a little as he speaks. He looks as if he has no idea whether to offer me a handshake or a hug.

"Don't be silly." I pull him into a tight embrace. I can feel the raised flesh of the burns beneath his shirt as I hold him close. "You are *not* intruding."

As we move toward the table, I take his hand and show it to Tanner. "Look. The birthmark."

Tanner nods. I told him about it last night, somewhere between our burgers and our milkshakes. Kole knew already, of course, but listened intently all the same.

"Did you recognize Nova?" Mack asks, bringing over the coffee pot.

Nico sits back down and scrapes his fingers through his dark hair. I take the seat opposite him. "Not at first, but now…" He smiles at me and takes my hand across the table. "Now, I know exactly who she is."

"We have so much to catch up about," I say, taking a coffee mug from Mack and blowing across the top of it to cool my drink. "When did they take you? *How* did they take you? How did they even know about you? Should I call you Sam or Nico?" The idea that I might finally have someone in my life who shares a piece of my past—someone who could help me remember the way our parents laughed, the meals our mom cooked, the music they listened to on Sunday afternoons— is making me talk too fast and too loud.

Nico opens his mouth to answer but Mack interjects. "First, *we* have some catching up to do too." He leans on the table. His shoulder muscles tighten beneath his hoodie. "Nova, we need to learn everything we can about what the League is doing."

"Of course." I put my mug down. My mouth feels suddenly dry.

"You need to tell us everything you saw, everything you heard, even the smallest details." Mack glances at Nico. "But not here. After breakfast? If you're up to it."

I nod. He doesn't trust Nico yet and that's okay. He will when he realizes what I've realized—that Nico is a piece of me I thought I'd lost—he'll grow to trust him.

"Where's Kole?" I ask Tanner.

"Still sleeping. How are your powers?" Tanner runs a hand over my arm and slots his fingers through mine.

"Returning, I think." I turn my palm upwards and concentrate hard. A spark splutters to life. Not as strong as normal.

"Kole consumed more of Eve's poison than you. It'll be a while before he's back to full strength." Tanner stands, downs his coffee, and says, "Nico? Why don't I show you around while Mack and Nova talk?"

Nico looks uneasy. "I thought… breakfast?"

"Let's get you washed up first. You've been down here all night." Tanner puts a firm hand on Nico's shoulder. I feel like asking him to go easy, but instead, I nod and tell Nico, "It's okay. Go with Tanner. We'll talk this afternoon."

In the doorway, Nico stops and turns back to me. "Nova? I'm glad I'm here. Even if it happened in a scary way, I'm glad we found each other again."

I hug my waist and smile at him. "Me too. I'm glad too."

* * *

As soon as Nico leaves the room, in true sheriff mode, Mack takes Nico's seat and puts his hands palm-down on the table. "Nova, first things first, you cannot just blindly trust Nico. I know he's a celebrity, a familiar face, and I know they told you he's your brother but—"

"Mack, it's more than that. Don't you think I'd know if he was a fake? I see it in his eyes. He's *Sam*. He's *my* Sam."

Mack's jaw twitches. "You last saw your foster brother when he was six years old."

"He has the birthmark."

"Where has he been all that time?"

"He was taken into foster care, a different one from me. He was adopted. He—"

"Nova," Mack clutches my hands and dips his head to hold my gaze. "He has the birthmark, that's a fact. Everything else is what you've been told." He sighs and strokes my hand with his thumb. "I want this to be true. I want you to have your brother back, but we need to make sure he can be trusted before we tell him *anything* about you, or the prophecy, or what's been going on here. Okay? We have to be careful what we say around him until we're absolutely certain he's on our side."

Emotion throbs in my chest. I know Mack's right, but at the same time I feel like pounding the table with my fist and yelling, *Can't I just have one thing?! Can't one thing from my past just turn out to be not as horrible as I thought it was?!*

"Okay?" Mack nudges my chin with his index finger. His eyes are deep and hypnotically brown, flecks of gold making them look amber in the morning light.

"Okay." I sit back in my chair and fold my arms in front of my chest. "Okay."

Mack nods and breathes out heavily. Then he takes out his phone and turns on the voice recorder. "Luther's out looking into Nico. It's tough. Town isn't a safe place for us right now, but he has some contacts who might be able to help."

I bite my lower lip. I don't like the idea of them prying into Nico's life, not after what he's been through, but if that's what it takes to show the guys that he can be trusted, then I won't object.

"In the meantime, let's talk about what happened. If you're up to it."

I inhale slowly and take a long sip of coffee. "I'm up to it," I tell him. "But first, I need you to promise me something."

"All right."

"Did Luther tell you what I did to Johnny?"

Mack blinks at me but doesn't seem fazed or disgusted. "Yes."

I close my eyes, pushing back the memory. "Then I need you to promise that you'll teach me how to control it. The fire. Because I can't ever lose control like that again." I lock my gaze onto his so he knows I mean it. "Ever."

"I'll teach you," he says. "I promise."

"And we'll start today." It's a statement not a question.

Mack hesitates for a moment then says, "Yes, we'll start today. After we've been through everything you learned about the League and their plans."

34

MACK

"She doesn't know much." I pour myself a glass of whiskey, even though it's not long past midday, and offer Luther one too. He shakes his head, but Kole takes one. I don't bother to ask Tanner; he hates the stuff.

Through the window, we can see Nova talking to Nico by the fountain. The fact they're alone out there makes me twitchy. But if they move out of sight, one of us will follow.

"We didn't see much," Kole says, talking about the forty-eight hours they spent in captivity with H.E.L.. "I could identify a couple of the werewolves but there were at least fifty watching Eve's little show. Too many to remember them all."

"But we know now, for certain, that the League was behind Johnny's video," Luther says.

I nod. "And that the entire thing was, exactly as we thought, a distraction so they could capture Nova and test her."

"Which means they suspect she's The Phoenix, but they need to be sure of it before they kill her?" asks Tanner, the word 'kill' heavy on his lips.

"Or that they don't want to kill her," Kole says. After a

pause, he adds, "Perhaps they want to turn her." He looks down at his arm. There's a small puncture wound where the witch inserted her needle. He came within a whisker of having F.H.B. pumped into his veins, and the close shave has left him rattled. If there's one of us who I'd never have expected to be overpowered like that; it's Kole. When he looks back at me, he takes a large sip of whiskey from his glass and says, "Ever since I accessed the prophecy, we've known that Kayla isn't top dog. She's second in command. The guy in charge is the one who wanted it so badly."

"The guy with no name," I mutter, still pissed that after all this time we have no idea who the highest-up member of the organization is. Maybe we would have if the Bureau hadn't shut us down so fast.

"The guy with no name," Kole agrees. "We know he's not a demon, but the prophecy is about *stopping* a demon opening up the underworld, right?"

None of us speaks. Kole's had plenty of time to think this through over the past two days, and he knows the Human Extinction League better than any of us.

"So…" he downs the rest of his drink, "what if the League's Number One is supposed to find Nova and kill her… stop the prophecy so his best demon buddy can take over the earth and destroy all of humanity."

I narrow my eyes. Where's Kole going with this?

"*But* he's not quite sure yet whether he's going to keep his end of the bargain. Maybe he's planning on turning on his buddy. Pumping Nova full of F.H.B. and running his own bid for Master of the Universe."

"Kole," Luther says, "that's a big leap."

"It's a lot of guesswork," I add. "But…"

"They didn't kill her." Kole looks at each of us in turn. "Okay, they were testing her. They wanted to be sure she was The Phoenix. But why not just kill her anyway? Why not just finish anyone they suspected of being the one who'd stop the prophecy?"

There's silence for a moment. Tanner looks nauseous every time Kole mentions killing and Nova in the same sentence.

"It's a theory," I say eventually, one hand in my pocket, the other gripping my glass. "It's a good one, but it's just a theory."

"And either way," Tanner says, his voice more high-pitched than normal, "whether they intend to kill her or turn her, they'll come for her again now that they've seen what she can do."

Each of us nods solemnly.

"Should we leave?" Tanner asks, looking around the room. "Find a safe house somewhere? Go back to the cabin?"

I scratch my beard and try to think logically. Usually, I know what to do in these situations. But anything concerning Nova and her safety seems to slow my thoughts, make me unsure of myself.

"Right now, town is pretty safe," Luther says, answering for me. "Ironically, the heavy police presence and the hordes of reporters are creating a nice little barrier for us. So…" he hesitates, not wanting to tread on my toes, but I nod for him to continue, "I say we stay put. Ramp up our reinforcements. The four of us are here now, so we can lock this place down nicely. I'll keep investigating Nico." His jaw twitches. "My foray earlier resulted in nothing useful, but we need to know who the fuck that guy is and if he's really Nova's brother."

"And I'll try to make the Bureau see sense." From their response so far, I'm not sure of my chances. They've never believed in the prophecy, at least not enough to prioritize it over the bad P.R of having a witch try to kill a human.

"What about Eve?" Kole is now perched on the arm of the couch. He's gripping his glass. "Eve is powerful. More powerful than any witch I've encountered. If the League comes for Nova again…"

"We need to know how we can stop her," Tanner says.

Kole nods in agreement.

"You two need to rest." I put my arm around Tanner and rub his shoulder. He still hasn't spoken about the jump or how it made him feel. He seems normal enough, but there's something in his eyes that tells me he's not quite himself. He needs to digest it. He needs to reset. "You've both been through a lot."

"We can't just—" Tanner tries to object but I squeeze his shoulder.

"Watch Nova. Take care of her." I look at Kole. "We need you both fighting-fit for what's coming."

Tanner closes his eyes and turns away from me but Kole nods. "We don't know how long we've got," he says.

"Right." I down the last of my drink. "Then we have some reinforcement spells to cast."

* * *

I'VE JUST GOT off the phone from an asshole junior agent at the Bureau when there's a knock on my study door. I grunt for whoever it is to come in, but when Nova appears I shake my head and say, "Sorry. Not a good time." I gesture to the phone. "I was trying to get the Bureau to see sense. They won't talk to me. They've got agents arriving in town tomorrow. Told me to wait until then."

"It'll be okay, Professor." Nova leans on my desk and smiles at me. She looks tired, but still unbelievably beautiful. Mid-afternoon light filters through the shutters and makes her hair shimmer. "I'm safe here with you all."

I want to believe that's true, but after what we've learned about Eve, I'm not so sure. Right now, we don't know how powerful she is. For all we know, she might be able to simply click her fingers and dismantle the protection spells we cast on The Hollow and walk straight in here.

"Are you ready?" she asks, standing up.

"Ready?"

She looks at her hands. "You said you'd teach me." Her eyes widen. She's asking me because she's scared— scared of herself and scared she won't be able to defend herself.

I glance at the phone. I should call the Bureau back and yell some more but would it achieve anything? Probably not.

Snow grumbles at me. It's almost a purr. He wants to help Nova. Of course, he does.

"Okay," I say, standing up forcefully. "Alright. But this time, we'll skip the books. We don't have time for you to learn about the history of magick or the laws of the elements. We're just going to… wing it."

Nova tilts her head. A smile flutters on her lips. "*Wing* it? Is that a pun?"

I narrow my eyes at her.

"Wing? Bird? Phoenix?"

"Oh." I push my fingers through my hair. "No. It was just a fifty-year-old professor-turned-sheriff trying to sound *cool*."

"If you want to sound cool… don't say 'cool,'" Nova giggles.

"Noted." I walk over to the shutters and flick them closed. When I turn back to her, she's standing in front of me. In the half-light, her figure is tantalizingly curvy. Her breasts, her hips, the swell of her thighs. *Shit*, I thought it was only Kole who had this much trouble being around her.

"We're doing it in the dark?" she asks, moving closer.

Why does everything she says sound like an innuendo? I swallow hard and clear my throat. "I need you to focus."

"Okay." She shakes her arms and moves her head from side to side. "Focus on what?"

I step closer. She's shorter than me. She fits perfectly under my chin. Small but full at the same time. "I need you to focus on what you feel." I place my hand on her stomach. "Here." She flinches but doesn't push it away. "And here." I put my other hand on her chest. Above her heart. Above the tattoo that covers her scar. "Emotion is the key to elemental power. You have to learn to manipulate it. *Use* it to help you bring the heat when you need it and extinguish it when you don't."

"Sounds easy," Nova says sarcastically. Her heart is beating faster than usual. I can feel it beneath my fingertips.

"Which emotions make the fire come?" I ask, keeping my hands on her.

She closes her eyes. "Anger, fear, grief…" She hesitates.

"What else?"

Her eyes open. She fixes her gaze on mine. "I always get… hot… when I…"

"When you…?" I search her face. Her skin is getting warmer. I can feel it through the fabric of her thin sweater.

She leans into my touch. "When I have an orgasm, sparks fly. Literally."

Now my breathing is heavy. Snow is pacing. He releases a frustrated groan that passes my lips as a murmur. "Has that always happened?"

Nova tilts her head.

"Before you came to Phoenix Falls, had it happened before?"

She laughs again and shakes her head. The movement makes her chest rise into my palm. "The first time it happened was when I hid under Kole's desk and heard him fucking Tanner."

The matter-of-fact way she says this makes me hold my

breath and count to ten. If I don't calm down my erection will soon be pressing into her thigh. I'm trying to *teach* her for fuck's sake. Trying to help her protect herself when the time comes.

"Alright." I force myself to step back. I turn and face the window, exhaling quietly and slowly, trying to think of anything except how badly I want to make her spark like that.

When I turn back, I'm wearing my 'professor' face. "So, let's use the opposite of those emotions to calm the fire down. Alright? Ready to give it a try?"

* * *

FOR ALMOST THREE HOURS, Nova relentlessly practices casting flames and extinguishing them. She wants to keep going. She wants to know everything about elemental affinities, and secondary affinities, and spells, and potions. But she's exhausted. I can see it in her face.

"Nova. We can do this again tomorrow. I can't teach you everything in one day." I brush her elbow— the closest I'll allow myself to get after the way I felt with my hands on her body. "You did great."

For a moment, she looks like she's going to object. But then she says, "Alright. Thank you, Mack."

"Tanner will be itching to see you." I gesture to the door. "Go show him your new tricks."

As she disappears and the door closes, my heart beats faster. I release a loud sigh, stand up, and pace the room. Snow is growling. He wants me to give in to the torrent of lust inside me, but I can't. *I'm old enough to be her father*, I tell him.

He growls louder.

I stalk to the bookcase and lean on it, trying to bury the

multitude of inappropriate thoughts that are barreling through my body.

The way she looked at me when I was teaching her… I wanted to lift her up, wrap her legs around my waist, and smash her up against the wall. Or bend her over my desk. Or lay her down in the middle of the room and kiss every inch of her perfect flesh.

The pants she was wearing hugged her hips in a way that made my dick twitch and my balls pulse. But they were the pants I lent her. *Layla's* pants. Which makes me one sick bastard doesn't it? Thinking about fucking a girl who's wearing my dead sister's pants?

Snow grunts at me as I thump a large hardback book and send it crashing to the floor. He thinks I'm being an idiot. They're just pants. They look good on her. It doesn't mean I think she's Layla. I loved Layla. I didn't *ever* think of her that way. She was my sister. Nova is not my sister, or my student. She's a woman. A gorgeous, curvaceous, goddess of a woman. Living in my house. Making love to two of my best friends. Making noises that travel up through the walls and cause them to shake.

She's a beautiful, powerful woman who—if she learns to harness the power inside her—could crush any of us just by looking at us. Thinking about what she did to her filthy scumbag ex-boyfriend makes my veins light up with arousal. The idea that she could overpower him like that…

I can't take it anymore. I pull my dick from my pants and fist it, hard. I need to come. I need a quick, dirty release.

I lean on the shelves, tugging fast and rough as I picture her sucking on my balls then spreading herself for me.

A rush of air makes me stand up and turn around. The door is open. Nova is standing silhouetted inside it.

Her eyes travel the length of my body. When they reach

my erection, my hand still wrapped around it, they stop. She steps into the room. The door closes.

She doesn't move. Neither do I. "Don't stop," she says, meeting my eyes.

I don't even try to resist.

I stand, legs apart, facing her and move my hand slowly up and down my shaft.

"That's not how you were doing it before. Show me how you were doing it before." She steps closer. She folds her arms as if she's bored with waiting.

So, I give her what she wants.

I jerk my dick as hard as I can and as fast as I can. When I'm about to come, I close my eyes, but she says, "Look at me."

I do as I'm told. I hold her gaze and spray ropes of hot cum onto the floor between us. She watches me. Then she glances at the desk, says, "Forgot my phone," picks up the cell I hadn't even noticed, and walks away.

35

TANNER

After supper, Nova goes to bed. She doesn't want to go alone, but I need to catch up with Mack. Luther's AWOL, and I need to know if he's found anything yet on the guy *claiming* to be Nova's brother.

I hate the idea of Nico being in close proximity to her. They talked all morning and more after her lesson with Mack. She believes he's Sam. She *wants* to believe it. But ever since my time with the League, I've never trusted werewolves. And this one especially seems too good to be true.

"How did she do?" I ask Mack as soon as Nova's left the room.

He blinks at me. Is he blushing?

"The lesson? Are her powers back to full strength?"

Mack stands up, hands in his pockets. A pose that always makes me feel as if he's about to deliver a lecture. "I'm not sure we even know the extent of her full strength yet, but yes, she's got them back. She did well. But it's child's play compared to what she'll need to do to fight off Eve." He rubs his beard. "We'll need a bigger arena for her to practice. We need to skip the small stuff. What she did to Johnny... that's what we need her to do to the wolves."

"We can't push her too hard." I look out toward the fountain. At this time of night, watching it always makes me want to swim.

"We need to push her, Tanner. For her own safety." Mack leans on the door frame. It's approaching fall and the evenings are becoming increasingly cold. He glances at me. "But how are you? After the jump..."

"I'm fine." I shrug and look away. I'm not fine. I'm anything *but* fine. But I don't want to talk about it.

Mack lets it drop. "And Kole? His injuries?"

"He's healing and his powers are returning, but I haven't figured out what Eve gave them to mute their abilities. Do you have any books that might help us narrow it down?"

Mack nods. "I'll check the study." He's about to say something else when a bone-rattling scream shakes the building.

In unison, we start to run.

36

NOVA

I'm somewhere very dark and very quiet. It's cool and peaceful. My skin tingles. Something is coming.

I turn around but all I can see is darkness.

Then there are lights up ahead.

I walk toward them. But they're not lights, they're eyes. Wolves. Blinking at me through the night.

I try to back away but there are more behind me. A huge black wolf with sapphire blue eyes and a flash of blond fur down its back prowls toward me. It bares its teeth.

I hold out my hands and whisper, "Stop, please," but the wolf keeps coming.

They've got me circled.

So many I can't count.

My heart hammers. My breath quickens. I try to scream but I can't. Fear turns to icy terror and freezes me to the spot.

Then the wolves pounce.

* * *

I sit up in bed, drenched with sweat, shaking. The door flies open. Nico rushes in and pulls me to his chest. "Are you okay? What happened? You screamed. *Really* screamed."

"I couldn't..." I mutter. "I couldn't scream."

I can still hear the wolves growling. My head is pounding. I screw my eyes shut and push Nico away from me. I stumble out of bed and rush to the window. I need air. Cold air. I throw it open then slide down the wall and sit with my arms around my knees.

I don't feel fully awake but I'm not asleep anymore either.

Mack and Tanner rush in.

"I think she had a nightmare," Nico says. He's shirtless, wearing nothing but boxers, and looks like he was in a deep sleep himself. "She's not talking much sense."

Tanner crouches in front of me. "Nova?"

"Wolves," I whisper. "I saw wolves. They were coming for me."

Tanner smiles a little and strokes my hair. "It's okay. It was just a bad dream." He turns to look at the others. "I've got this."

Mack nods at him and leaves. Nico hesitates. "I could stay," he says to me. "If you want me to."

"I've got this," Tanner repeats tightly as he pulls me to my feet.

"It's okay, Nico. I'm okay," I say as Tanner guides me back to the bed.

Nico bites his lower lip. "All right," he says. "But you know where I am if you need me."

When the door closes, I fold myself into Tanner's arms and let the sound of his heartbeat ground me. "I'm sorry."

"What are you sorry for?" he asks, dipping his head to smile at me. "After what you went through, bad dreams are to be expected."

I breathe out slowly and rub my arms. The breeze from

the window is now too much. Tanner closes it and pulls a throw from the headboard, wrapping it over my shoulders.

"Wait there, I'll make you some tea." He moves to stand up, but I grip his hand.

"No, stay. I don't need tea. I need you."

He kisses my forehead and slides into bed, pulling me to his chest.

"Where's Kole?" I ask, wondering why he didn't come when I screamed.

"He could sleep through the apocalypse," Tanner chuckles.

"And Luther?"

"Out playing detective. Went back to the hotel to see if he can find anything useful."

I nod, although the thought of him returning there makes me shudder.

"It's okay." Tanner hugs me tight. "You're okay."

For a moment, I let myself close my eyes and breathe in Tanner's scent. I rest my head on him and try to push back the fear that's still swirling in my stomach even though the dream is over. "You don't like Nico much, do you?" I ask, sitting up a little.

Tanner wrinkles his nose. "I don't *not* like him."

"But you don't trust him around me?"

"I don't know him well enough to make that judgment call yet." Tanner bites the inside of his cheek. "But I can't say I'm a fan of sharing your affection." He smiles cheekily and nuzzles my neck.

"That's not true at all!" I laugh. "You've shared me quite happily with Kole."

Tanner frowns. "That's different."

"How?"

"Because Kole's like a brother to me."

"A brother you sometimes fuck?" I ask, tilting my head.

"You know what I mean." Tanner rolls his eyes. "It's different."

"How?" I ask again.

"It just is." Tanner looks a little pissed now. He's pouting and it's super cute.

I sit up and wriggle my toes. "What about Mack? Are you jealous of him too?"

"Mack?" Tanner's eyebrow twitches. "What's there to be jealous of?"

I bite my lower lip. What happened in Mack's study didn't feel like enough of a something to mention, but suddenly I want to know what Tanner will do when I tell him. "I walked in on him earlier." I tuck my hair behind my ear, heat fluttering in my core as I remember. "He was… *enjoying* himself."

Tanner frowns but then his eyes widen. "Jerking off?"

I nod, feeling like a schoolgirl sharing secrets. "Right after our lesson. I went back for my cell phone, and he was just standing there with his dick in his hand."

"Really?" Tanner rolls on top of me and slides down my body so his chin is resting between my tits. "And then what happened?"

"Nothing." I shrug. "I told him to keep going, so he did. I watched him come, then I left."

Tanner thumps the bed and laughs. "What?! Poor old Baloo. You just left him?"

"He won't give in." I push my fingers through Tanner's hair, stroking it away from his face. "He wants to, I can feel it, but he won't let himself. He thinks he's too old for me."

Tanner makes a *pfft* noise with his lips. "He's fifty-two, not eighty-two."

"Exactly." I fold my arms, suddenly feeling aggrieved. I look at Tanner. His eyes are sparkling. He *likes* that Mack wants me. "So, Nico bothers you but Mack doesn't?"

"I know Mack. I trust him." Tanner sits up but doesn't allow the conversation to steer back toward Nico. "He deserves some happiness."

I nod. Tanner's talking about Mack's sister.

"I have an idea, Little Star." He leans in and presses his nose to mine. Conspiratorially, he says, "I have a feeling you're going to struggle to sleep tonight. So, why don't we play a game with our professor instead?"

"A game? What kind of game?"

37

MACK

Leaving Nova when she looked like that was almost impossible. Snow almost took over. She was terrified. Wide-eyed. Desperate for comfort.

But after my near-miss earlier, I didn't dare to stay.

Knowing Tanner's probably soothing her right now, kissing and licking and touching all the places that will stop her from feeling afraid, I lie back in bed and stare at the ceiling.

I stay like that for a while, trying to meditate. Trying to empty my mind of Nova. Then I give in and start getting ready for sleep.

When I'm finished in the bathroom, I take off my hoodie and slacks and put them back in the dresser. I'm about to take off my boxers too when the door clicks.

I look up. "Tanner? Is Nova all right?"

Tanner leaves the door open and steps inside. He shakes his head and sighs. "She's pretty shaken up."

I'm about to tell him it's understandable when he moves aside, and I realize that Nova is right behind him.

"I am *very* shaken up, Professor." She closes the door

behind her and trails her gaze from my chest to my shorts. "I'm not sure I'll be able to sleep." She inches closer. "I need a distraction."

I almost laugh and tell the two of them to quit playing games, but she's wearing nothing but a black vest and panties. No bra. Her breasts full and loose. And Tanner's watching her with a glint in his eyes.

She walks over to me and slots her fingers between mine. Her chest is pressed against me. My dick is already paying attention.

Reaching up on tiptoes, she brings her lips to mine. I close my eyes. I'm about to back away when her warmth disappears. She tugs my hand. She's leading me to the corner of the room. To the large gray armchair by the window.

Forcefully, with heat in her palms, she pushes me into it. Then she clicks her fingers.

Tanner strides over and reaches behind his back. He pulls out a piece of fabric and hands it to Nova. Then he takes another from his pocket.

While Nova ties my left hand to the chair, Tanner ties my right. I don't resist them. I should, but somehow the fact Tanner is here too makes me feel like it's safe for me to let them take control.

When they're done, Nova turns around and peels off her vest. As it inches up her back, and her creamy skin is exposed, a sigh rattles my throat.

She drops it to the floor. The sides of her breasts are only just visible. I want them in my hands. I want to roll her nipples between my fingers.

Next, she bends over and removes her panties. The curve of her ass makes my mouth go dry. I breathe slowly but don't take my eyes off her.

"Let me help you." Tanner takes her hand and, as if he's helping a princess into a carriage, lifts Nova onto my lap.

Her ass lands firmly on my crotch. She wriggles it a little, and a groan escapes my mouth. I expect her to pull me free and slide onto me, but she doesn't. She lies back, using my chest to support herself, and loops her arms up around my neck, jutting her breasts out.

Tanner leans over her and lowers his mouth to her nipple. He draws his tongue over it, then sucks it into his mouth. He teases her. Licking then stopping, licking then stopping, so that she wriggles and squirms.

My balls throb with arousal. I need to adjust my cock. It's bulging beneath her ass, but I can't reach it and she doesn't seem to care that every time she moves, it makes me twitch.

Tanner is moving lower now. He plants a row of kisses across her stomach, over her belly button, and hooks her legs over the arms of the chair.

The backs of her thighs press against my arms.

He looks up at her as he kneels, then says, "One second," rushes to the bed and returns with a pillow. Putting it beneath his knees, he grins and says, "I intend to be down here a while. Might as well be comfortable."

Nova laughs. The vibration rumbles against me. Then she tilts her head back and moans as Tanner's tongue starts working her clit.

I can't see what he's doing. All I can see are her breasts, her thighs, and the top of Tanner's head, but the sounds she makes as he laps and sucks and toys with her make me growl and tug against the restraints.

"I'm going to come, Tanner... don't make me come." She reaches down to grab his hair and pull him back up her body. "I want to come around your cock."

Tanner grins. His lower lip glistens with Nova's juices. She looks at him and runs her finger across his mouth, then she stands up and turns around so she's facing me.

She holds up her finger and leans over, her breasts

dangling onto my chest. She puts her lips to my ear and whispers, "Does Daddy want a taste?"

Fuck. Holy fucking shit. *Daddy?* Where did that come from?

My eyes roll back in my head. Every muscle in my body wants to rip free from my restraints but, at the same time, I'm enjoying the torture. I want to come, but I want her to keep teasing me first. And I want her to call me that again.

She meets my eyes and tilts her head. "I thought you'd like that," she whispers. "I thought you'd like me to call you Daddy while you taste my pussy."

I open my mouth, letting her finger inside. It's the only part of her I can taste, or feel, so I suck on it like I'm ravenous. Holy hell she tastes good.

Behind her, Tanner has been fisting his dick, but now he smooths his hands over her ass and opens up her legs. She looks down at me. She's bent over, about to take Tanner's dick into her cunt but she's looking at me.

As he enters her, she lets out a small mewing sound and closes her eyes. She bites her lower lip as his cock strokes her inside walls. He gives it to her slowly at first, but then she speeds up the rhythm, grinding back onto him.

Her breasts move back and forth in front of me. I open my mouth, praying I'll catch a nipple between my teeth, but she doesn't let it happen.

"Do you want to play, Daddy?" she asks, cupping one of her breasts and toying with her own nipple.

I can't answer. I nod.

"Say please." She lowers her lips to mine and moans into my mouth.

"Please." As soon as I say the word, Tanner whips my arms free. I reach up, hold her waist, smooth my thumbs over her breasts, lean into her neck and run my tongue across her throat. I try to grab my boxers and pull them down, but Nova catches my hands. "Ah ahh," she says, "I said you could play with me. Not yourself."

I groan as she reaches back and, through my boxers, gives my balls a sharp tug.

Tanner quickens his pace. He's making circles with his hips. Nova thumps the back of the chair and yells, "Fuck, yes, Tanner! Don't stop."

He brushes his hair from his face. His chest glistens with sweat. He curls an arm around her waist and pulls her back onto him harder and harder.

"Daddy, I need your help." She takes my hand and leads it to her core. Her wetness makes me growl. As she leans on the arms of the chair, I sit up and apply pressure to her clit. I make slow, perfect circles. Her eyes widen. She bites her lower lip then she jerks upward and stops breathing as her entire body convulses with an orgasm.

Tanner comes at the same time. He moans into her shoulder and bites down, leaving small indents in her perfect skin.

He holds her for a moment. She's breathing so hard that her breasts shake.

She kneels down in front of me and tugs at my boxers while she's still shaking. I roll them over my hips, and my erection pops free.

She examines it, smiling, then flicks her tongue over the slit. It's dripping with pre-cum. She laps it up. Then she draws a long sharp line with her fingernail from my base to my tip.

It's a sensation I've never felt before.

She tugs on my balls at the same time and the mixture of pain and pleasure makes me groan. This is what I needed. How did I not know this was what I needed? She looks up at me. "Do you think it will fit, Daddy?" she asks, moistening her lower lip.

"She's a good girl," Tanner says, smoothing Nova's hair from her face and grinning at me. "I think she can take it."

Nova swirls her fingernail across my shaft for a second time. I cup her face in my hands. "Please, stop teasing me. Please, Nova."

She blinks at me, smiles, then finally takes me in her mouth. All the way in. Her body jolts when I hit the back of her throat. She grips my thighs. And that's all it takes. She knows I'm coming, and takes her mouth away, sitting back on her heels as she and Tanner watch me shoot cum onto my own stomach.

I drop back into the chair, shaking.

Tanner helps Nova to her feet. She leans over me and kisses my forehead. "I knew you'd give in eventually," she says softly. "Don't you feel better?"

I shake my head but start laughing. Feel better? Fuck, I haven't felt this good in years. I'd forgotten how to feel this good. I bring her to me so I can kiss her. "Yeah, Supernova, I feel better."

38

NOVA

When Kole finds Tanner and I in Mack's bedroom, he looks as if he's going to leave. But I beckon him over to the bed.

"Please," I tell him. "Stay with me. All of you." I'm so tired. So very tired.

As Mack pulls me into his chest, Tanner rests his head on my stomach, and Kole curls around Tanner. Their warmth is soothing, like a lullaby.

"I don't want to fall asleep," I whisper. "I don't want to dream again."

Mack strokes my hair. Tanner kisses my naked stomach. Kole finds my hand and squeezes it. "It's okay, Little Star," Tanner says. "Sleep. We're here."

I yawn and close my eyes. I'm drifting away when I feel all three guys lurch upright. There are footsteps on the stairs. Urgent footsteps.

Mack wraps his arms around my waist and pulls me to him. Tanner and Kole jump in front of me. Kole glances at a small potted plant on Mack's windowsill. Its leaves start to grow, a small stem turning into a snake-like vine. His power is returning.

Tanner holds a ball of water in his hand.

The door clatters open.

"Nico?" I nudge Tanner aside, somehow not embarrassed to be naked and wrapped only in a sheet—despite the fact Nico is my brother. "What happened?" I tug the sheet with me and climb out of bed.

The guys don't relax.

"Have you seen it?" he asks, his eyes wide.

"Seen what?" I glance back at the guys. In unison, they get up.

"Another video." Nico is holding his phone. He passes it to me. "Nova, it's bad. Really bad."

Tanner and Mack appear at my shoulders. Kole is behind me. I lean into him as I press play.

I watch only a few seconds before I drop to the floor, sobs wracking my body.

"Shit. Shit. Shit." Tanner has grabbed the phone and is staring at it.

"Don't watch it," I beg him. "Please don't."

Mack stoops down, picks me up, and carries me to the bed. He sits me down and rubs my shoulders. "It's all right, Nova."

"How is it all right?" I look at him through the tears that are misting my eyes. "I'm a murderer. They have it on camera. I made him *explode*."

Kole shoves the phone back at Nico. "You thought it was appropriate to show her that?" he growls.

"What the fuck were you thinking?" Tanner adds, squaring up to Nico.

"I just... I thought she deserved to know." Nico backs away. "The whole country was out for blood when they thought she *attempted* to kill a human, but now they have it on camera that she..." he searches for the word, "*'flayed'* her ex-boyfriend from the inside out. 'Boiled his blood.' Whatever else they're calling it."

"Shut the fuck up." Tanner lurches for Nico. His hand goes straight to his throat. Kole doesn't stop him.

"Stop!" I shout, jumping up from the bed. "Stop it! All of you!"

"Did you do this?" Kole asks, glowering down at Nico over Tanner's shoulder. "Were you in on it?"

"How... would... I...?" Nico stutters, grabbing at Tanner's hands.

"He's been with us the whole time, how could he?" I shout as I try to pry Tanner's hands away from Nico's neck.

"It's clearly the League." Mack strides over, puts a hand on Kole's shoulder, and nudges him away. To Tanner, he says, "That video had to come from security in the hotel. Nova's right, Nico's been with us the whole time. It can't have been him."

Tanner wavers then relaxes his grip and throws Nico to the floor.

I kneel beside him.

"Nova..." Nico puts his hands on my arms and looks up at me. There are red finger marks around his throat. "This isn't right. You being here. It's not safe. We have to go."

"Nova needs to be with us," Tanner growls.

Nico ignores him. "I have money. I have contacts. Come with me. Come away with me and I'll take care of you." He pulls me into his arms and holds me tight. "I'm your brother. I'll take care of you."

39

LUTHER

I'm just through the tunnel and heading back to Phoenix Falls when my phone rings. It's a number a don't recognize. I ignore it. The hotel was a dead loss. Too many cops and Bureau agents. Not a single werewolf or H.E.L. member in sight.

I send a voice note to Mack. "No luck here. What about Pete the vamp? He was in on Kole's kidnapping. Might have intel. Can Tanner locate him? Or is another jump a bad idea?"

When I'm done, the phone rings again. This time, when I read the number, something snags in my brain. I recognize that dial code.

Ridgemore.

I pull over and reverse dial. The phone rings five, six, seven times. Then finally someone answers.

"Hello? Who is this?" I ask sharply.

"Is that Luther Ross?" A shaky voice on the end of the line asks. It's a woman. Older than Nova. Maybe in her sixties or seventies.

"Who's this?" I repeat.

"My name is Sarah. Sarah Borello." Her voice grows a little stronger.

"Okay, Sarah Borello, how can I help you?"

"I'm from Ridgemore."

I don't say anything, just wait.

"I know Nova."

Now, that's got my attention.

"I was her neighbor for a long time. I helped her escape the night she burned down the apartment."

"Okay, so what do you want? If you're trying to extort money or favors, you're better off trying the press."

"No, no, it's not that. Please..."

I lean closer to the phone. She sounds desperate. Sincere. Scared. "Sarah? What is it you want to tell me?"

There's a long pause then Sarah says, "Nova's foster brother, little Sam... he's alive."

I grip the steering wheel. "Nova's brother is alive?"

"Yes," Sarah whispers.

"And how do you know this?"

She sucks in a deep breath. "I know because I saw him at the hospital after the fire, and I saw them take him away."

"So, it's true. They put him in care and just never told Nova..." I mutter, shaking my head. I can't fucking believe it. Nico was telling the truth.

"In care?" Sarah says. "No. No, you've got it wrong. Sam wasn't taken into care. He was sent away. They took him away."

"Who took him away?"

"The League." Sarah's voice trembles.

"You're telling me Sam is *not* now going by the name of Nico Varlac?"

"The werewolf?" Sarah scoffs. "No!"

"And you have proof of this?"

There's a long pause. "Of course, I do. I wouldn't have

risked calling if I didn't. Sam's..." She stops, exhales loudly, then lowers her voice. "I know where he is. I can take you to him. Meet me at the diner on route thirty-five. Between Ridgemore and Red Rock. I'll tell you everything I know."

"Sarah—"

"Tomorrow. Eight a.m."

"Sarah…"

The phone goes dead.

LOVE BLAZE?

If you enjoyed Blaze, I would be incredibly grateful if you'd leave a review so that others can discover it too!

As an independent author, reviews are one of the most important tools we have to help spread the word about our books.

Even if it's short, it will be *hugely* appreciated.

Simply visit Amazon, Goodreads or StoryGraph, search for The Phoenix Prophecy, and hit 'leave a review'.

THANK YOU

Thank you for reading Nova by Cara Clare. If you are looking for more books to get lost in please check out our other published titles at;

www.apbeswickpublications.com.
A.P Beswick Publications
Oswaldtwistle Mills Business Centre
Clifton Mill
Pickup Street
Accrington
BB53AP